The Crooked Knife

A Claire Burke Mystery
(Book 2)

by
Emma Pivato

This book is fiction. All characters, events, and organizations portrayed in this novel are the product of the author's imagination or are used fictitiously. Any resemblance to actual persons—living or dead—is entirely coincidental.

Copyright © 2014 by Emma Pivato

All rights reserved. No parts of this book may be reproduced or transmitted in any form or by any means, electronic or mechanical, including photocopying, recording or by any information storage and retrieval system, without written permission from the author, except for the inclusion of brief quotations in a review.

For information, email **Cozy Cat Press**, cozycatpress@gmail.com or visit our website at: www.cozycatpress.com

COZY CAT
PRESS

ISBN: 978-1-939816-35-1
Printed in the United States of America

10 9 8 7 6 5 4 3 2 1

This book is dedicated to my husband, Joseph Pivato, in appreciation of all his encouragement and support over the past 40 years. My life would have been very different without you, Joe—and not nearly so good!

Acknowledgements

I thank my friend, Patricia Brunel, for providing additional background information on Barbados.

I would also like to thank Bruce Uditsky, Chief Executive Officer of Alberta Association for Community Living, for providing me with additional information on the AACL mandate.

Chapter 1—Marion's Dilemma

Marion Mackay was nervous. After a lifetime in Calgary, she was moving to Edmonton to live with her married daughter. At age 75, and with arthritis and a gradually worsening heart condition, she did not feel she could manage alone in her home any longer. She remembered when her husband had been struck down by a heart attack seven years before and she did not want to be alone if that happened to her. Nor did she want to move into a 'Supported Living Residence,' as they were euphemistically called, with a bunch of strangers.

Leaving her family home, the home she'd lived in most of her life since she was a small child, was one thing. Moving to a different city where she knew nobody but her daughter and would not be able to navigate around on her own was another. But the part that made her the most nervous of all was not the move, upsetting as that was. It was the prospect of moving her nephew.

Bill Mackay, now 33, had become Marion's responsibility when her brother and his wife had been killed in a car accident 18 years before. Bill, their only child, was autistic. He was fifteen when they died and becoming difficult to handle. Marion knew she and her husband could never manage him, and had found an emergency placement at the Forbes Centre, a Calgary institution for the care and management of individuals with developmental disabilities unable to care for themselves. Bill had been there ever since and she visited him faithfully once a week and sat on the Patient-Family Counsel. It met monthly to discuss various ways to improve services and to lobby against the funding cuts that the provincial government tried to introduce from time to time. And recently, this lobbying had become an even bigger battle because of their threat to actually close the institution, now seen to be out of step with current notions of normalization and inclusion.

It had taken Bill a solid year to adjust to the loss of his parents and his life as he had known it. Any 15 year old would have been traumatized, but Bill was also dealing with a limited capacity for understanding and an autistic rigidity that made change of any kind extremely difficult. But now he had been at Forbes for eighteen years and had grown comfortable there. Marion knew that moving him at this point would be very upsetting and she had struggled hard with the decision. There was no other family to share the responsibility with and she had finally concluded that her brother and sister-in-law would not want her to leave Bill alone in Calgary.

After her husband died and she was all alone, Marion had thought that she would like to move to Edmonton someday to be near her only daughter and she had put Bill's name on the waiting list for the Clive Centre in Edmonton six years ago. Last week she had received a call that a vacancy had become available. She had been given just two weeks to arrange the transfer or the spot would go to the next person on the list and Bill's name would go to the bottom. *But how can I possibly tell Bill?* Marion asked herself.

During Bill's first year at the Forbes Centre, a combination of teenage hormones, his autistic resistance to change, and pain and disorientation over the loss of his parents had caused him to become very violent at times. Marion recalled those scenes with dread: the physical and chemical restraints, the lockdowns, and the threats of expulsion. Behavioral issues had continued intermittently but in the past few years Bill had seemed to mellow. She worried that all this hard won adjustment would be lost when he moved again.

Bill always seemed happy to see Marion when she visited and they had a relationship of sorts. But it appeared that he'd developed a closer relationship with a couple of other men in their 30's who'd been assigned to his table at mealtimes, and six months ago a woman, also in her 30's, who'd been placed at his table. Her name was Mavis. She was in a wheelchair, could only mutter indistinctly a few words, and was unable to feed herself. Yet Bill had become fascinated with her. He called her Mae-Mae and Marion was very much afraid that he would not want to leave her behind.

Mavis' brother, Jimmy Elves, flew down from Edmonton every two weeks to visit her, and Marion wondered if she could get him to accompany her and Bill back to Edmonton by car. It would be much faster to take the plane but she did not know how much Bill would act out. It could be very embarrassing or worse. The pilot might do an emergency landing somewhere and he could then be kicked off and turned over to authorities. No, it would have to be the car, but she couldn't risk going alone with him. And anyway, he would be confused and might need help in the bathroom when they stopped for breaks, help neither she nor her daughter could give him. In any case, her daughter wanted no part of moving Bill. She thought he should just stay at Forbes. Surely Jimmy would agree to help her. She must phone him. He was due for his next visit in three days.

Marion did not know when to break the news to Bill and this worried her constantly. Once she told him he would just start obsessing over it. On the other hand, she could not just jerk him out of there at the last minute without giving him a chance to say good-bye to everyone. And staff would probably want to arrange a party for him. Already the time was too short for that. What to do? What to do?

Chapter 2—The Move

When Jimmy Elves picked up the phone and Marion identified herself, his anxiety rose.

"Marion—is Mavis okay?"

"She's fine, Jimmy. I'm calling about Bill." Marion explained the situation and asked for Jimmy's help with the move.

Jimmy was not a forthcoming kind of person. In fact, he often appeared to others to be a little on the surly side. He also tended to get wrapped up in his work as an electrician and to resent any disruption to the flow of his everyday life. But he remembered all the years he had counted on Marion to keep an eye on Mavis and keep him up to date on what was happening at the Forbes Centre.

"Okay, I can do that," he replied slowly. I'll change my plane ticket to a one-way and we can drive back together in your car, Marion." Marion let out a long sigh of relief and thanked him profusely.

When the phone call ended, Jimmy sat down with a cup of coffee and considered the situation. Once Bill and Marion were gone from Calgary, he did not see how he could leave Mavis there at Forbes alone. And now he did not have to. His wife, Megan, had resisted any suggestion that Mavis should come to live in Edmonton. But she'd been murdered six months previously and that had changed a lot of things for Jimmy. They had not been close and Jimmy had been suspected of her murder by the police. However, some new friends had worked hard to find the real killer and clear his name—and they'd succeeded! Jimmy smiled when he recalled all their antics. The interior designer his wife had hired had been the one to find Megan's body but it was the positive way in which her multiply-disabled daughter, Jessie, had responded to Jimmy that had convinced the designer Claire and her friend, Tia, of his innocence. When Jimmy thought of Tia, his smile took on a bitter-sweet quality. *Such a funny person*, he thought. *She was so proud and yet so defensive. And what a worker*! She had come into his home to clean and had done that wonderfully—but her real goal had been to snoop. The snooping was a search for clues to the killer but when Jimmy finally heard about it, he had been furious and the relationship between him and Tia had been touchy ever since.

As arranged, once Jimmy arrived at Forbes in Calgary and had a brief visit with Mavis, he and Marion met together with Bill to tell him the news. Predictably, Bill became very anxious and his first clear thought after he managed to calm down a little was about Mavis.

"Mae-Mae. Not leave Mae-Mae. Mae-Mae come too. Mae-Mae come too." With that, Bill started rocking back and forth in his chair, faster and faster.

Jimmy struggled for the right words to calm him, promising that he would bring Mae-Mae up to Edmonton for visits and that someday soon she would even live there and they could see each other all the time. He had said this because he knew it was what Bill wanted to hear, but even as he said it, Jimmy realized it was true. Somehow, he was going to have to bring Mavis to Edmonton and find a way to take care of her there. Once when he'd still been in touch with Tia during the murder investigation, he'd mulled over this possibility with her and she'd offered to help him if he ever decided to do that. But now they had not talked in a long time and probably her plans had changed and she had moved on.

Chapter 3—The Clive Center

"Mae Mae come soon?" Bill kept asking all the way to Edmonton. But other than that, the trip was surprisingly uneventful. Marion was still worried though—about how Bill would react when he got to the Clive Center and had to meet all those new people.

They arrived in Edmonton about three in the afternoon and drove to the Clive Center on the North side. After some back and forth negotiating at the check-in, they were buzzed through and told to take the elevators to the third floor and to go to Unit 3-A. Someone would be expecting them there. Bill liked elevators so that made the trip up easier—except he did not want to get off. Jimmy took him by the elbow, talked about Mae-Mae (he had given up calling her Mavis in front of Bill) and said how he was looking forward to bringing her to live in Edmonton. Bill was somewhat mollified by his soothing tones and walked readily enough into the unit after they were once again buzzed in. Obviously, the security here was tighter than it was at the Forbes Centre where Bill had not been in a locked unit.

Sharon, the floor nurse, greeted them warmly and, addressing herself to Bill, said, "We've been looking forward to meeting you, Bill. We have your room all ready. Would you like to see it?" Bill made no reply but together they all trooped down the hall to the room assigned to him, Jimmy carrying both suitcases. It was a smallish room with one window that looked out on a wall three feet away. If you looked to the side, between the two buildings, you could just see a part of the front lawn and the road leading into the Centre. Bill sat down on the bed and started to rock. "Where Alan bed? No Alan bed. Need bed for Alan."

"Alan's in Calgary, Bill," Marion replied in a gentle voice. "He's at Forbes. This is a new place. You and I are going to live in Edmonton from now on."

"No, I go back to Calgary. Calgary good. Calgary my place"

Sharon said, "Well, I'll leave you to get settled in, Bill. Dinner's in half an hour." She turned to Marion and Jimmy. "You're welcome to stay for dinner if you wish. It might help Bill to feel more comfortable."

"Thank you," responded Marion, gratefully. "I'll just start putting away his things now. Where should we go for dinner?" Sharon told them where to go and after she left, Jimmy pointed out the washroom to Bill and asked him if he would like to use it and wash up before dinner. Then he did the same. Meanwhile, Marion organized all of Bill's scant possessions neatly in his drawers and closet. She placed his clock radio on the night stand beside his bed and plugged in the nightlight he always insisted on having on at night. Then she showed him his Gameboy. "Look, after supper you can play with this for a while before bed! I bet you are going to be tired tonight after that long drive!"

Bill made no comment. He just stared ahead numbly.

At dinner, the three of them shared a table with another young man in his early thirties whose name was Josh. They tried to talk to him although he did not speak back. Bill, too, had been very non-communicative since arriving and continued to be so but with the support of Jimmy and Marion, he got through the rest of the evening uneventfully and was settled into bed at 9:30. Marion arrived at her daughter's home about ten and was shortly in bed herself, exhausted.

The next day was Sunday, but Marion was at the Clive Center by ten in the morning and did not leave until nine that evening. Bill spent most of the day alternately rocking and playing compulsively on his Gameboy. Over and over he asked for "Mae-Mae." By Monday morning, Marion was really feeling the strain. She had a sore throat and her daughter, Hilda, insisted that she sleep in. At 11 o'clock, Hilda drove her mother to the Clive Centre.

When Marion and Hilda arrived, it was to discover that Bill had had a major meltdown at breakfast. He'd been roaming around the dining room in an agitated state and had struck out at a nurse who had bossily ordered him to remain sitting at his breakfast table and tried to pull him back there. He was now confined to his room for lunch and was sitting on his bed rocking violently when they came in. Bill did not seem to recognize Hilda whom he'd not seen in several years and he hardly seemed aware of Marion's presence. All he said over and over was, "Want Mae-Mae. We go home now." This upset Marion very much and she felt that she had made a terrible mistake bringing him there.

Chapter 4—An Unfortunate Phone Call

Marion was in bed by nine that night, feeling worse than ever. Hilda had insisted that they leave the hospital at the dinner hour, citing Marion's health as her reason. However, it was obvious that Hilda could not stand to be there any longer and was becoming more bored and irritated by the minute. Marion went to sleep feeling very sad and alone.

At six the next morning, Marion was awakened by the jangling of the phone. When she picked it up she could hear much scurrying and agitation in the background even before anyone spoke. Her heart pounded in those seconds waiting for a response. Once the caller had determined that she was talking to Marion, she identified herself as Judy Odin, the charge nurse on duty in Bill's unit, and informed Marion that a serious incident had occurred during the night. The nurse Bill had had the confrontation with the morning before, had been found stabbed to death in the hall near Bill's room when a nursing assistant was beginning the morning bed check prior to the seven o'clock shift change. When Bill's room was checked, a bloody knife was seen on top of the coverlet on Bill's bed where he was apparently sound asleep. The police had just been called and were on their way. Bill was still sleeping. The nurse had thought it better not to disturb him.

After taking a few moments to absorb this information, Marion replied, "I'll call a taxi now and be there as quick as I can. Please wait until I'm there to wake him if you can. I'm his guardian and should be present before anyone talks to him." The nurse agreed with this and hung up. Marion was shaking but she quickly called the taxi, washed and dressed. She wanted to call Claire. Claire would know what to do if anyone did, but the taxi honked its horn outside. She saw Hilda's purse on the chair, grabbed her cell phone and her own purse, and left quietly. She did not want to wake Hilda and deal with what she would have to say.

Once inside the taxi, Marion groped inside her purse for Claire's number in the little address book she carried. Then she tried to call her but could not make the phone work. She asked the driver to help her, explaining it was urgent. He pulled over and dialed the number. The phone rang three times before a gruff, sleepy voice responded. It was Dan, Claire's husband. Marion had never met him.

"Hello, this is Marion McKay. I'm sorry it's so early but it's an emergency. I have to talk to Claire right now."

"I don't know who you are. What's this about?"

"Please." Marion was sobbing now. "Please. I need help"

Just then she heard Claire's voice on the other line. She'd awakened and slipped into the kitchen to answer the extension. "Marion? Marion McKay? What's wrong?"

"Claire, Claire, please come to the Clive Centre and help me. The police are on their way. They think Bill murdered a nurse. I have to protect him. I know he could not have done it. Please help me. I don't know how to deal with them." Marion was crying openly now and her heart was pounding.

There was a pause and then Claire said, "I'm on my way. Don't let them talk to him until I get there. I know the address. I can be there in 15 minutes. Please try to calm down, Marion. It's not good for your heart."

"Okay," Marion said weakly. She handed the phone back to the driver to close it since she was not sure what to do and leaned back exhausted against the seat.

The driver gave her back the closed phone and then said, "This Bill guy you're talking about. Is he a client or a nurse? I know people in the Clive Centre".

Marion was happy to talk. She needed to talk just to quiet her racing heart if nothing else. "He's my nephew and I'm his legal guardian. We just moved here and we are all alone and I'm all he has and I just know he's innocent," she babbled.

"Well, why do they think he murdered someone then?"

"They found a bloody knife on his bed where he was sleeping."

"He was sleeping?"

"Yes, that's what the nurse said. It was only six when she called and they had just discovered it."

"Why would you kill someone, crawl into bed, place the knife you used on top of the sheets and then go to sleep?"

"Well, when you put it that way it doesn't seem to make much sense—but he's autistic."

"My son is autistic and he's in the Clive Centre. I think I'm going to park the car and go in with you!"

"Oh, that would be great! I feel so shaky I'm not sure I can make it up the stairs."

"Is he on the third floor? That's where my son is!" The driver was really getting agitated now and seemed to be driving faster. In two more minutes they were there. Marion fumbled with her purse but he waved impatiently at her and grabbed her arm. They hurried up to the third floor and to Bill's unit. They rang the bell and the charge nurse let them in. She looked surprised to see the man with Marion but recognized him right away.

"What are you doing here, Len? Geordie is fine."

"I was driving this lady in my cab, Judy, and when I heard what had happened, I thought I better come. Are you sure Geordie is okay?"

"Yes, none of the clients are up yet and they don't even know what happened. I am just waiting for the police. I thought you were them."

Just then the doorbell rang again. Judy opened the door to find a dapper, fortyish man waving his badge at her. He strutted in and introduced himself as Inspector McCoy and his taller, less trim, but kinder looking partner as Sergeant Crombie. "What's going on here?" McCoy demanded.

Judy took a step back, a frequent response to McCoy's brusque manner. "One of our nurses was stabbed to death. I don't know exactly when."

At that point, the doorbell rang again. The nurse opened it to admit Claire, and Marion ran to her. Claire wrapped Marion in her arms. McCoy turned and recognized Claire. "What are *you* doing here?" he snarled. Claire blanched when she recognized Inspector McCoy. They had clashed frequently a few months previously when Jimmy's wife had been murdered and Claire and her friend, Tia Ambrose, had set about finding the killer.

"Marion is a friend. She asked me to be here for support. She's Bill's guardian but you can see the state she's in—and she has a heart problem." This last was said in a warning tone, since from past experience Claire was certain McCoy would do his best to bar her from Bill's room. Only the threat of a possible liability issue down the road would soften his stance.

"You may accompany her then but do not interfere and do not talk!" McCoy glared menacingly at Claire for emphasis. Behind him, Sergeant Crombie caught Claire's eye and winked. While McCoy had been nasty and resistant to their help during the murder investigation for the killer of Jimmy's late wife, Crombie had secretly admired the efforts of Claire and her good friend Tia to track down the killer and had discreetly assisted them whenever he could.

They entered Bill's room together, Claire trailing behind with her hand lightly on Marion's back. What they saw was a surreal scene you might expect in a movie—Bill, still snoring gently, flat on his back with the bloody knife lying on his chest and his right hand wrapped around it. Claire quickly but quietly removed her hand from Marion's back, extracted her cell phone, and took several pictures before McCoy realized what she was doing.

"Here," he bellowed. "You can't do that! Delete those pictures at once!"

This sudden harsh noise woke Bill. He looked at them and then down at his chest. He saw the knife and flung it violently across the room. Meanwhile, Claire had converted to video on her phone camera and was still filming, but McCoy was so mesmerized by this sudden act that he did not notice.

"So much for fingerprints," Crombie groaned, but he still put on gloves before picking the knife up and placing it carefully in an evidence bag. McCoy was watching him which gave Claire the opportunity to place the phone at the bottom of her purse out of sight and hopefully out of mind for the moment.

Bill had become very agitated and Judy, the nurse, came in and asked them to leave. Marion begged to stay and Judy assented but briskly ushered the rest of them out. The taxi driver was still waiting in the reception area and the pathologist had just arrived to examine the body. McCoy's attention turned to him and the driver turned to Claire. He gave her his card. "Please tell that lady if she wants any help with all this to just call me. I got to know this place is safe for my son."

Meanwhile, McCoy and Crombie watched as the pathologist examined the body sprawled face down in the hall outside Bill's room. Claire quietly stepped over close enough to hear what he said. It did not take the doctor long to reach some preliminary conclusions. "Death is due to one stab wound to the back. No signs of a struggle or other injuries. By the looks of the blood pool beneath her, she died where she's now lying. Her body temperature places time of death between four and six this morning."

McCoy had assigned a policeman to stand guard outside Bill's door and not to allow him out. This was causing him to become more and more agitated which made it hard for any of them to focus. "The forensic technicians should be here in about ten minutes," Sergeant Crombie told McCoy.

At that moment, a heavy set, middle aged woman approached them and introduced herself as the unit manager Ivy Watson. "When are you going to take him away?" she asked. "We can't keep a murderer here."

"It's not clear yet that he is the murderer, ma'am," Sergeant Crombie started, "and…"

McCoy interrupted. "We'll be shipping him off to the dual diagnosis unit at Wild Rose Hospital right away. We can't stick people like him into the general jail population. Crombie, make the call!"

"But…" Crombie started to say.

McCoy was about to interrupt him again when Claire jumped in. "Wait a minute," she said assertively. "You better take a look at these pictures before you do that."

"I told you to delete those pictures!!" McCoy snarled.

"I can't. They are evidence—and, anyway, I have already sent them to my computer and I think I'd better send them to you as well. That way, you will have them and you will understand why Bill's lawyer will be challenging the murder charge and calling for a dismissal in court." Crombie was again behind McCoy's back and he smirked.

"What are you talking about? Not that this is any of your business in the first place... The evidence could hardly be more incriminating." Behind McCoy's bluster was an almost hidden note of fear. He had been on the wrong side of Claire before and had not come out of it too well.

"I'll show you if you're interested." McCoy said nothing and Claire, taking this as an invitation, moved over between him and Crombie and showed the first picture she had taken. There was Bill sleeping and the knife arranged almost vertically down the middle of his chest with his right hand clasping it. "Bill is strongly left handed. I checked with Marion."

"That doesn't prove anything for somebody like him!" McCoy blustered. "He's crazy!"

Claire gritted her teeth but could not stop herself. "Go ahead and say that in court," she blurted. "The advocacy movement for people with developmental disabilities in Edmonton is very strong. This case will get tried in the papers and not only will you lose, you will come out of it looking like an ignorant bigot!"

As soon as she'd said this, Claire rued her words. McCoy could be a formidable enemy. But then the nursing unit manager, who had been quietly listening to this exchange, spoke up. "She's right, you know. I've seen more open and shut cases than this get set aside. Those people will have a field day and will milk it for all the publicity and public sympathy they can get!"

This was not exactly the kind of support Claire had wanted since she was one of 'those people,' but she managed to keep her mouth shut this time, reasoning "any port in a storm."

But then the woman continued. "Whether he did it or not, he's agitated and we can't keep him here. Just look what happened on that bus from Edmonton to Winnipeg when that schizophrenic guy cut off a man's head! He has to go. I want him out of this facility by noon. Where you put him is up to you."

"Wild Rose Hospital is the only place that's going to take him. Make the call, Crombie," McCoy ordered. "And then get the detectives busy questioning all these people and establishing timelines and alibis."

Marion was allowed to accompany Bill in the ambulance and Claire followed in her car. He still seemed dazed. Marion was also quiet, sitting beside him and just rhythmically rubbing the middle of his back in small, circular motions. She knew from past experience that moving her hand any higher, towards his shoulders and hence closer to his head, would just agitate him. She also knew better than to talk, recognizing the peculiar, shut-down state he was in and knowing how he could suddenly break out of it with the energy of a coiled snake if triggered.

Chapter 5—New System; New Rules

At the dual diagnosis unit they were met by the unit manager and the charge nurse and ushered into a small conference room for the intake process. Marion sat beside Bill and held his hand but when, in answer to their questions, she stated that he had come from the Forbes Center where he had been for 18 years, Bill jumped to his feet almost tipping the table over in his agitation.

"Mae-Mae. Where Mae-Mae? I go home now. Want to go home!"

Just at that point, Claire entered the room, having been delayed by the need to find a parking place and then getting directions to the unit and then convincing staff that she needed to be part of Bill's intake process. She saw the look that passed between the nurse and manager and anticipated what was coming—sedation. Quickly she sat down beside Bill and gently touched the middle of his chest to get his attention in a non-threatening way. "Bill, Mae-Mae is coming. She's coming soon, maybe tomorrow. She's coming and you won't be alone. Mae-Mae is coming, Bill. Mae-Mae misses you. Mae-Mae will be with you." Claire droned on like this in a hypnotic voice and Bill gradually calmed.

"Mae-Mae tomorrow?"

"Tomorrow, soon. You be patient. Mae-Mae coming. You stay here now. This place better. That other place no good for you. We don't like it. We don't want you there. This place good."

"This place good? This place good. This place good." Bill started an autistic rocking and repetition process that helped to soothe him somewhat.

"We go see your room now, Bill?" Claire looked inquiringly at the manager, silently pleading for understanding of the delicate calming process in which she was engaged. But it was the charge nurse who got the message first. She stood up and with a nod from the manager, turned to Bill.

"Go see your room, Bill?" she asked mildly.

Bill got up meekly to follow her. Claire got up, too, and touched his chest again gently to focus him. "I come with you? Marion stay here and talk a little while? Then she come. Okay?"

Bill did not respond but also did not object so Claire took his hand and they left with the nurse. Claire looked back over her shoulder and saw the manager nod a confirmation and smile briefly.

The room had two beds and Bill immediately said. "Allan come. Bed for Allan."

The nurse looked at him and said, "Maybe Allan will visit you but that bed is for Jim. You will like Jim. Jim is nice—like you. This bed is yours."

Bill said nothing but sat down on the bed the nurse had pointed to. Claire sat on a chair beside him but not too close. An orderly arrived at that point with Bill's suitcase and hand luggage. Claire could see that the false calm was about to end and noted a familiar bump in the carry-on bag. She opened it, pulled out his Game-Boy and handed it to Bill. "Show me game, Bill. I want to learn." Bill focused on the Game-Boy, muttering to himself, and gradually became immersed in it.

Twenty minutes later, Marion joined them, looking white and shaky. She walked over to Bill, hugged him and started to cry. "I'm so sorry, Bill. I'm sorry we came here. I thought it was best. I love you. I just want you to be happy and safe. I'm sorry. I'm sorry. I'm sorry."

Bill looked confused and started to agitate. Claire joined them in a group hug and then gently peeled Marion away, quietly pinching her in the process in a not too discreet message to suck it up. Then she started all over again reassuring Bill. "Marion did right. This place is *good*, Bill. You will like this place. That other place no good for you but this place good. Mae-Mae is coming soon, Bill. Then you'll be happy."

Bill did not look convinced so Claire continued. "Bill, you remember Jessie?'

"Jessie," Bill said. "Jessie little. Jessie chair like Mae-Mae".

"That's right, Bill. You remember. You want Jessie to visit you?"

"Jessie come today?"

"Later, Bill. I bring Jessie later today. You stay with Marion. Be good and play your Game-Boy. After you eat supper, Jessie will be here." Claire looked at the nurse who nodded agreement.

Once Claire sat down in her car, she realized how exhausted she was. She put her head down on the steering wheel and just sat like that for several minutes. It had taken every ounce of her energy to forestall the blow-up that she knew had been imminent and the sedation and vicious cycle that would have inevitably followed. She only hoped that Marion and the staff would follow through and keep Bill calm. Marion had regained control of herself by the time Claire left and by the admiring looks she had received from both Marion and the nurse, Claire felt that her role modeling had been recognized and appreciated and that it would be emulated. Right now, though, she had other tasks to perform. First of all she had to contact the Alberta Association for Community Living and explain the situation to them and get their help. She dialed their number and was fortunate enough to be able to get right through to their Chief Executive Officer, Bruce Uditsky.[i]

Once she heard his voice, Claire felt her own energy surge back. Here she was on familiar ground with someone who could understand and empathize with what was going on with Bill. She quickly explained the situation, gave Bill's history including his occasional aggressive outbursts, which within the context of autism were very common. They stemmed primarily from an inability or very limited ability to accurately perceive and respond to social cues. People with autism were not by nature anti-social. There were, of course, those individuals with autism who had been chronically misunderstood and badly treated and reacted accordingly, but that was not what had happened to Bill. He had been loved and well cared for by his family and respected and understood for the most part by his aunt and by the people at the Forbes Center. He was not mean or hateful at all and the only times when he lashed out were when he was in situations that he did not understand and could not cope with.

Bruce Uditsky understood that typical characteristic of autistic functioning very well. He agreed with Claire that Bill needed and had a right to an informed advocate and mentioned a retired man whose autistic son had passed away a few years earlier. Marvin Gale continued to volunteer with the association to help fill the empty space left by his son's death, and had made it a point to attend disability education workshops and meetings so that he had the skills necessary to function as an effective advocate. He drove and since he actually lived in the same sector of the city as the hospital it would not take him long to go back and forth there. Bruce also mentioned a criminal lawyer willing to work for a reduced rate in situations like this and who would probably relish the challenge.

"I am not sure about Marion's finances," Claire responded. "She is retired and living on a pension. And Bill has nothing but his AISH that I am aware of."

"Don't worry too much about that," Bruce assured her. "AACL can assist with covering the costs of a criminal lawyer or even fully cover them if necessary. We have worked with several criminal lawyers through the years and they have done excellent work with the clients we have sent them who had criminal charges pending against them. However, if we do assist, AACL would want to remain engaged in offering strategic input to the lawyer in terms of our knowledge of people with autism and how they are likely to respond in situations like you describe."

"That would be great!" Claire replied enthusiastically.

"Okay, I will get back to you as soon as I have contacted these two individuals. Meanwhile, tell Marion not to worry. She and Bill are not alone. And tell her she did a wise thing moving Bill to Edmonton. We can offer both of them a lot of support. And I will also contact the Autism Society and ask them what resources or support they might contribute. I will arrange a connection with Marvin and he can work with them directly to funnel support to Bill and Marion."

It was a long way from Wild Rose Hospital to Claire's home in South West Edmonton and by the time she arrived there, it was already four in the afternoon. Jessie had returned from school and her after-school assistant was there for her 4-8 shift. Claire greeted Jessie who seemed mildly happy to 'see' her. Actually, twelve year old Jessie could not see or at least not in the usual way since she had cortical visual impairment. That is to say, she could not process the image coming through her retinas in a meaningful way. But she was certainly aware of Claire's presence since all her other senses, and particularly her hearing, were finely attuned. Claire told the assistant what was happening and asked her to get Jessie ready to leave as soon as she had finished supper and used the commode. Her second set of range of motion stretches would have to be sacrificed tonight for the sake of the greater good and the assistant could leave early with full pay. This last incentive galvanized Amy into action and she began working more quickly and efficiently than was her usual style. Claire watched her for a minute and just shook her head. Then she went to find her husband, Dan, and explain the situation to him.

Dan was, as usual, not very sympathetic. He was always very protective of Jessie and was frequently exasperated by the way Claire dissipated her energies on various sad causes, feeling, with some justification, that they had enough on their own plate. But Claire was not prepared to back down on this. She grimly served up a selection of leftovers for supper, eating little herself, and soon left the table to see how Jessie was coming along. As usual, the assistant had forgotten to put on her AFO's (ankle foot orthotics that helped keep Jessie's legs and feet in alignment). Also, there was an ugly food spot on her sweater. Claire sighed in resignation. "I will finish getting her ready. Would you please go and load our supper dishes into the dishwasher and clean up the kitchen? Then you can leave."

"I guess I can do that," Amy replied, her tone being that she was doing Claire a favor even though she was being paid for an extra hour. Claire gritted her teeth but said nothing but a meek "thank you."

Claire and Jessie did not get to Bill's room at the hospital until 20 to 8. Nothing was ever fast where

Jessie was concerned. Claire hoped they would be allowed to remain until at least 8:30 and that Marion could last that long. Claire would be driving her home and would save the details of her conversation with Bruce Uditsky for the drive so she could focus the time available on Bill and Jessie and facilitating their interaction.

A different nurse came into the room just after Claire entered with Jessie. Claire braced herself for starting over from square one and justifying their presence there but the nurse interrupted. "Oh, Bill, this is the young lady to visit you I have been hearing about! Well, you have a nice visit." Turning to Claire she added, "I am Alma, Bill's nurse tonight. If you have any questions or problems just ring the call bell. And don't worry about the visitors' sign. Stay as long as everyone is comfortable. We are not a sick ward, after all!" With that, she turned and left. Claire was vastly relieved and focused on developing a relationship between Bill and Jessie.

"Do you remember Jessie, Bill? You met her in Calgary at the Forbes Centre."

"Jessie," Bill responded, and he reached over and touched her chair. "Mae-Mae chair. Where Mae-Mae?" Mae-Mae come?" Jessie smiled tentatively.

"Soon, Bill. Jessie wanted to meet you. She wants to have a new friend. Can you be her friend?" But even as Claire said the words, she realized how wrong they were, how patronizing. Did she really think that one person in a chair could replace another with whom Bill had developed a special relationship? Talk about stereotyping! And could she really justify dragging Jessie up to this place, new and strange to her, and on a school night? What about *her* rights?

Caught up in her thoughts, Claire was uncharacteristically silent. Bill looked at Marion.

Marion looked at Jessie. Claire looked at Bill. Jessie just put her head down and began moaning, quietly at first and then with a high, keening wail. Bill covered his ears and began shuffling his feet.

"I think maybe we should leave," Marion finally said. Claire got up without a word and started the process of working Jessie's stiff arms into her jacket and fastening all the straps that would ensure she was secure in her wheelchair once they were in the car. This was always a tedious task but tonight she was almost glad of it. They soon said their good-byes and headed back to the car. Thanks to the innovative 'Golden Boy' Swinger Lift, which had been developed and produced right there in Edmonton, and the small size of Jessie's chair, Claire was able to load Jessie despite the fact that a car had parked less than three feet away from the wheelchair van on the passenger side, oblivious, as most people seemed to be, to the wheelchair sign in the window and the fact that the van was parked in a Handicapped Parking spot.

Once they started driving, Jessie immediately calmed down, sensing she was on the way home. Marion said, "Claire, I don't know how to thank you for all you have done for Bill and for me today. We would both have been lost without you."

"Yeah, well this last effort wasn't too brilliant," Claire said dejectedly.

Marion say gently, "What you did this morning when we got there was wonderful, Claire. As for tonight, it is impossible to always know what will work for somebody like Bill. And just look at all the change and upset he has been through since we left Calgary. I think all he wants right now is just to know what is going to happen to him next."

With this speech, Claire regained some of her fire and energy. She related to Marion the conversation she had had with Bruce Uditsky, and Marion was predictably pleased and relieved to no longer be carrying the whole responsibility for Bill herself. Marion then related to Claire what she had learned about the unit. First off, it was an assessment unit and was not meant for long-term care. Secondly, they were planning to hold off medicating until they could complete the formal part of the assessment if at all possible. Third, the process was starting tomorrow morning with a visit from the unit psychologist at ten.

Chapter 6—A Different Kind of Assessment

Bill had a restless night and was agitated the next morning when the nursing assistant tried to lead him to the breakfast room. Edna, the nurse who had interviewed him along with the unit manager the day before, intervened and suggested that Bill just have breakfast in his room. A tray was provided and she sat with him a few minutes until he calmed down enough to eat. But the calm did not last long and within 20 minutes he was rocking violently and talking to himself. He was conducted to a safe room where he could not harm himself.

Bess Enright, the unit psychologist, entered the room a few minutes later and saw Bill sitting on the floor in the far corner rocking gently and banging his head lightly against the wall, which was padded and rubberized. When he noticed her, the rocking and banging increased. Bess sat down on the floor in the corner opposite him and started playing with the large ring of keys it was necessary for her to carry to access her office plus various locked wards. She moved them softly back and forth for a few minutes not looking at him. After several minutes, she slid them gently across the floor to him, averting her eyes in the process. After several more minutes of silence in the room, Bill slowly reached out and picked them up. He started jingling them and moving them round and round the ring. Bess sat silently for another ten minutes, watching him out of the corner of her eye. Once she saw that the activity was automatic and slowing down into what was for him a comfortable rhythm, Bess quietly opened her brief case and extracted a series of seven soft foam balls of different sizes and colors. They had a fuzzy surface and could stick together when stacked. For ten minutes she played with them, lining them up small to large and then large to small. She put them in a circle. Then she took a small plastic suction cup from her bag. She stuck it to the floor and then gently stacked the balls vertically on it: large to small and then, more daringly, small to large. Eventually, that arrangement tipped over. Out of the corner of her eye, she could see Bill watching the balls. She took them apart and then rolled the smallest one to him, again not looking at him directly. All this time she had not said a word.

Bill took the ball, felt it, rolled it, held it against his clothes to see if it would stick. It did not. Slowly, one at a time, Bess rolled the other balls to him, waiting each time for him to respond. She watched as he, too, lined them up and even made the circle. After another ten minutes of this, Bess moved across the floor and placed the plastic suction cup within his reach. Bill waited until she had returned to her corner and sat down. Then he slowly reached out and touched the cup. A couple of minutes later he took it and played for several minutes with it, finally succeeding in getting the suction cup to stick to the floor. He placed the big ball on it and then the next biggest but when he got to the third it fell over. He replaced it and it fell off again. Then, for the first time, he looked at Bess.

Bess took that as an invitation and slowly crossed the floor, again keeping her eyes down and on the ball structure. Settling once more on the floor she took the balls off the cup and slowly and elaborately lined them up so they were exactly even. This time the structure stood. Then she took all the balls off except the largest one and, again without looking at Bill, handed him the next largest ball. She pointed to the structure and pantomimed with her hands keeping the ball straight. Then she placed her hands limply at her side and just sat there. Bill's rocking had increased because of her nearness. Bess moved back a couple of feet but did not return to the wall this time. She continued to sit inertly.

Gradually, Bill's focus returned to the balls. He looked at the one he was holding in his hands and placed it dead center on the top ball in the structure. This was a natural behavior for him in any case, the previous off-center placement for him having been a mistake because of his generally wrought up condition. Bess waited. Slowly Bill placed the remaining balls on the structure and then relaxed against the wall looking at it. He turned in her direction. She nodded her head up and down, this time looking at his face but not directly in his eyes. Then she reached over and moved the structure in front of her and waited. Bill did not object.

Bess slowly took the structure apart and restacked it with the smallest ball on the bottom. She left it for a minute and saw that Bill was closely watching. Then she took it apart again and moved the balls and the cup close to Bill. She sat back, about two feet away from him. Bill selected the smallest ball and placed in on the cup. Then he added the next smallest ball. It rolled off. Both Bill and Bess stared at the ball. After a moment she reached out her cupped hand. Bill looked at it and then looked at the ball. Then he looked at the cup with the small ball still stuck there. Eventually he reached over and handed the second smallest ball to Bess.

Bess looked at Bill but did not make eye contact and she nodded her head gravely while slowly moving over to the cup. She adjusted the smallest ball so the Velcro portion was exactly symmetrical on the top side and so it was firmly stuck in the cup. Then she stared closely at the second ball, tracing its Velcro patch with her finger.

Then, slowly and gravely, she placed the second ball on the first with the matching Velcro pieces exactly aligned. She looked at Bill until he gazed back at her and then she took the two balls apart, placed them beside the cup and moved away again.

After a minute or two, Bill reached out for the smallest ball and placed it in the cup. For the next hour, they continued this pantomime until Bill could match all the balls accurately and had lined them up, carefully balanced, small to large. Bess reached out slowly and patted him on the shoulder very lightly. "Good," she said in a grave, non-cheer leader voice. Then she gathered up all her equipment and stood up to go. "I will come back tomorrow, Bill," she said quietly. Bill said nothing but stared after her as she left.

Chapter 7—a Police Investigation of Sorts

Donald McCoy was a slender and smallish man but very dapper and very erect. His precise, gray-brown moustache, matching and closely clipped hair, chronically raised eye brows and flared nostrils gave him an air of authority and faint menace. Michael Crombie, his sergeant, was quite different. He was several inches taller and slightly overweight and with a growing paunch, he did not exude the same air of dignity as McCoy. Neither was there the sense of menace. His broad face was warm and friendly with one of those mouths that always seem to be slightly smiling, a welcome contrast to McCoy's perennial sneer.

The two men were sitting together, now, reviewing the notes that Crombie had taken about possible suspects in the murder of nurse Annette Richards and the events leading up to her death. "As far as I can see, the suspect list is very limited," Crombie began. "All I have been able to find out is the following. Annette was on night shift with two other staff members in that unit: LPN, Jennie Marlowe and nursing attendant, Frankie Jessick. It was a quiet night with all the clients apparently asleep peacefully. At 3:15 a.m. Annette told them she had a headache and was going to lie down for a couple of hours. She asked Jennie to wake her at 5:30 just in case the day charge nurse, who usually arrived at a quarter to six, got there early. According to Jennie and Frankie, this was not the first headache she had claimed to have at night and she was quite comfortable bunking down for a couple of hours and leaving the others to cope. This was against the rules, of course, but she was in charge and had made it quite clear that they could be quickly replaced if they did not cooperate and cover for her.

McCoy listened quietly to all this. He knew Crombie was quite capable of doing his job. "Go on," he said.

"Background checks on these two staff members provided no useful information. Jennie, the LPN, has only been at the Clive Centre for seven months. This is her first job after graduating from the two year Licensed Practical Nursing program at Norquest College. She is twenty-five and still lives at home with her parents. She claims not to have known Annette before coming to work there and stated that they do not socialize outside of work. Annette has been at Clive Centre for 18 months. She came to Edmonton from Barbados with her Canadian husband two years ago and began the job right after her work visa came through."

"Did you check on the husband?" McCoy asked. "The unit manager said she was married."

"Yes. His name is Norman Calder and he was also working a night shift—at the Esso plant in Refinery Row. He is an electrical technician. They have tight security there because of the El Qaida threats and several people have vouched that he was there all night including the security guards at both check-out points.

"Okay, what about the nursing attendant, then?"

"As it happens, Jessick is also from Barbados. But he only arrived here two months ago through the Foreign Workers program. He has been at Clive Centre since a week after that, once his paper work was cleared. They brought him over. He claims not to have known Annette before coming and when I asked him for his address there, I found out that his family lives on the other side of the island so their families were not likely to have had any contact with each other. Except for a smoke break he took around five, he stated that he was sitting at the desk with Jennie, the LPN, all night and she confirms that. He was gone about 20 minutes, the regular length of time for his break, and seemed perfectly normal when he came back, according to her. Jessick states that he did not see anybody else during his break so there is nobody to confirm that he was actually outside smoking.

"I was in Barbados for a holiday a few years ago," McCoy reflected. "It is a very small island. Hard to believe everyone does not know everyone else—or at least know of them."

"Do you want me to check further, sir?"

"No. Leave it for now. I still think the boy is our killer."

"You mean Bill, sir? He is actually 33, I believe."

"Whatever. You know what I mean."

Crombie knew, but he said nothing. He also knew when to keep his mouth shut.

"So that is it, then? No other suspects? No delivery boys, for example?"

"No deliveries before eight in the morning, sir. But there is one other possibility." Crombie told him about the adjoining 20-bed wheelchair unit. "They are supposed to keep the door between the units locked at night but they often forget and leave it open, including the night of the murder. In any case, all the staff had the combination. The locked door would only keep out the clients and they are all in wheelchairs and too disabled to wheel themselves. In that unit at night there is a registered nurse, two LPN's and a nursing attendant on duty. It has extra staff because of medical issues with some of the clients. I was able to get statements from all of the staff members, and to corroborate their whereabouts with each other."

"Go on," McCoy said.

"They do regular bed checks since their clients are more medically fragile than those in the unit Bill was in. The R.N., who seems to be, and is reported to be, a very serious, conscientious type, says that it is such a routine you can literally tell which room they're checking and how long they are there by the sounds of their footsteps in the hall. However, it was a very quiet night and one of the LPN's had gone for "a kip," as he put it. They do allow that because of their high staffing number. Anyway, that means that nobody actually saw him between 3:30 and 4:30 when he returned to the desk. Later, just before five, she says, the other LPN passed the room where he had been sleeping on her way to the washroom and she noted that the bed had been used. I checked his background. He is a Canadian and there is no evidence of any contact with the deceased outside of the workplace. And that is it, sir. There's nothing else to report at this time."

"Well, it looks more and more like Bill is our boy. You better contact the hospital in the morning and see what they have to say about him."

Chapter 8—a Collaborative Process and a Querulous Meeting

Bess, the psychologist, worked with Bill every morning that week for an hour or more. Once she had acquired a fair but necessarily rough idea of his cognitive capabilities and the extent of his verbal communication skills, she looked at those areas she judged most pertinent to the forensic investigation underway. What made him happy? What angered him? What motivated him? For the first two mornings she had asked Marion to come and fill out some questionnaire information: the usual autism inventories, an assessment of daily living skills and, perhaps most interesting, a personality questionnaire designed for nonverbal persons with lower levels of cognitive functioning.

The personality inventory had two forms, one for the client to fill out and one for a person who knew him or her well. Bill could not complete the form since he did not read but Marion did her best to complete the companion form. However, it soon became evident that there was much Marion did not know about what Bill felt and thought on a daily basis. The easy answer to this was that nobody knew because of the black box autism that separated him from the rest of the world in crucial ways. However, Bess was not satisfied with this. She contacted Carolyn James, the manager at the Forbes Centre in Calgary who was utterly shocked to hear what had happened. She vehemently denied that Bill would be capable of such an act and asked Bess to fax the personality and daily living skills questionnaires. She was going to arrange a special meeting for herself and two or three of the workers who knew Bill best to fill them out. She would also arrange a simultaneous conference call so off-duty workers who had developed a relationship with Bill could provide their input from home and so Bess could call in to provide the instructions and clarify any points of ambiguity, important for the proper completion of the forms.

During the subsequent conference call, everyone on line from Calgary expressed an equal degree of outrage and upset about what had happened to Bill and what he was being accused of, and they were only too glad to help. Two days later, Bess received the forms she had asked for along with a rich collection of anecdotal information on Bill's interests, behaviors and social interactions while at Forbes. This was like gold to her and she worked late that night quantifying where possible, and qualifying and providing vignette exemplars where appropriate.

Bess was a well-trained clinician and as such she understood the limitations of statistics and quantification in cases like this and respected that the real experts who could speak to Bill's abilities, motivations and personality structure were those people who knew him best. Her role with regard to dealing with this valuable input was to ask the right questions, provide the structure, correlate the information given with her own assessment results and then to write up the final report—nothing more. She worked hour after hour that Friday evening putting it all together and by three in the morning it was complete. She had done all she could do and the best she could do. However, just to be absolutely sure, she read it over again on Saturday morning and once more on Sunday evening, making some minor tweaks and adjustments each time and creating a one-page summary sheet which highlighted the most pertinent findings. On Monday morning she left for work an hour early in order to have time to run off copies and collect together some demonstration materials before the case conference at nine.

The case conference was held in a large room in order to accommodate the number of attendees. On one side of the table were Marion, Bill, Claire and Marvin, the AACL advocate Bruce Uditsky had arranged. On the other side of the table were the unit psychiatrist, Dr. Cheryl Milton, Bess Enright, the psychologist, and Alma Theron, who had been assigned as Bill's primary care nurse. Also present were Brian Evans, the occupational therapist, Ruth Moore, the speech and language pathologist, and the unit social worker, Ted Ramsey. The latter three were shuffling their own test forms which Marion had obligingly filled out to the best of her ability and apart from that they had had to rely on Bess for more direct and immediate information as to Bill's status since she was the only one of the professionals apart from Alma who had been able to form any sort of relationship with him. At one end of the table sat Donald McCoy and Michael Crombie. The lawyer Bruce had found for Bill had not been allowed to attend, although it would have made good sense to put all the known facts on the same table in front of the same people at once. But this was hospital policy where case conferences were concerned.

Dr. Milton began by introducing everyone and then explaining the purpose of the conference which was to share information and together determine whether or not it was necessary for Bill to remain in hospital for his own safety and that of others. If not, what alternate setting could be identified that would be appropriate for his needs.

At this point, Marion could not help blurting out, "But he will be going back to Clive Centre, right? He has no other place to go."

Ted Ramsey, the social worker, answered her. "Actually, it is my job to arrange placement upon discharge for any of our clients requiring it. I have been in touch with the manager at Clive Centre and she has told me very clearly that if there is any possible question remaining of Bill being the murderer he cannot return there. She has also told me that they can only keep the bed open for him for two weeks. If this question has not been settled satisfactorily by that time, the bed goes to the next person on the wait-list. They have a long wait-list, apparently."

Marion sat there stunned but said nothing more. The psychiatrist resumed with a list of the medications Bill had been on when admitted and her recommendations for changes and additions to this regimen in order for him to achieve more effective behavioral control now that the assessment period was over.

Alma Theron spoke next. As his key nurse, she had had more contact with Bill while he was in the hospital than anyone else including Bess so she had seen him in his various moods and interactions with others. She had seen him being sad or sensitive or shut down or reactive but never as aggressive or overtly anti-social.

Bess spoke next. She outlined the strengths and limitations in Bill's cognitive functioning but qualified that this was an approximation since formal testing was not possible. She then went on to describe his level of personality functioning, leaning heavily on the anecdotal information and observations of the staff members in Calgary who had worked with Bill over a long period of time.

As Bess reported, the Forbes staff remembered Bill as being, for the most part, cooperative and gentle but very limited in his capacity to communicate and to engage in meaningful activities beyond the automatic ones in his daily repertoire. Despite these severe limitations, almost all of them had commented on Bill's generally pro-social behavior. If people dealing with him became impatient and "got in his face" he could react by pushing them away and he did not seem to realize how hard he was pushing so sometimes he had actually managed to knock people over. But such incidents were so rare that only three of them were on record over the past 18 years and none of the individuals involved had suffered more than a couple of bruises.

Bess had asked for an incident summary and the manager had personally prepared it and emailed it up to her. Bill had never been observed to deliberately go after somebody or to act out of malice. The main emotions he showed when confronted with someone who clearly had no patience for or understanding of his autistic limitations were fear and aversion.

Bill had been observed to enter a room, see the person there and then back out and leave on several different occasions during the past year because Forbes had hired a staff person who never really caught on to the rhythm of the place and rubbed a number of people the wrong way. There was never enough evidence to dismiss her until one night fortunately she was caught stealing an industrial-sized roll of plastic wrap when she happened to run into the manager on her way out of the unit after shift. The staff members reported that all the clients seemed to settle down and be happier and more content once she was no longer there, implying that Bill's reaction had been quite normal.

Bess talked for about 15 minutes and the team listened patiently. Her skills were well respected and they knew that if anyone could provide the information needed to make a determination of the best course for Bill's future it would be her. Inspector McCoy tried to interrupt her on a couple of occasions but Dr. Milton put up her hand to stop him each time and told him firmly that he could ask questions of clarification only and those should wait until Bess finished speaking. By the time he had his chance, McCoy was quite frustrated and spoke in his best sneering and dismissive tone, causing Sergeant Crombie, seated beside him, to wince visibly. "That is all very well and fine, what you say but it really doesn't prove anything so it is not much good to us. All we want to know is if he could have killed that nurse."

Bess looked at him for a minute before responding. Then she said, "From my experience as a forensic psychologist I would say that anyone, including those around this table, could have killed that nurse under the right set of circumstances. Perhaps you should focus on finding out just what those circumstances were in this case. Did Bill have more than the initial confrontation with her reported in the file, for example? Had she rubbed other clients the wrong way also?"

McCoy bristled. "I don't need you to tell me how to do my job."

Bess responded, "And the sentiment is mutual." Somebody snickered but quickly covered the sound with a cough.

Brian Evans, the occupational therapist broke into the chilly silence that followed with his report. He stressed that Bill was solidly left-handed and had below average and measurably less hand strength, and fine motor speed and control in his right hand than in his left, according to the assessment measures he had completed with him.

Ruth Moore, the Speech and Language Pathologist, then followed with her report, speculating that it was likely that Bill had greater receptive than expressive language ability. However, she had been unable to do formal testing with a Peabody Picture Vocabulary Test or any other appropriate instrument because he would not or could not cooperate with her.

Dr. Milton then concluded the meeting by saying that the assessment process had now been completed and no behaviors had been uncovered which would be consistent with Bill having violent tendencies. As this was an assessment unit only, there was no reason for Bill to remain longer and he could be discharged as soon as an appropriate placement became available. The unit social worker would be conferring with the Clive Centre unit manager to see if Bill could return there.

Ted Ramsey turned to Marion. "Will you sign a release so I can share our psychology and occupational therapy findings with Ivy Watson immediately?" Marion nodded her head in agreement. "If Ms. Watson does not agree to take Bill back," Ted Ramsey continued, "I will be contacting PDD, the Alberta government department responsible for funding the agencies that provide staffing support for persons with developmental disabilities in Alberta. They will have to find an appropriate placement for Bill. He can't stay here much longer." Marion nodded glumly.

Inspector McCoy stood up at this point. "I'm leaving now. This information is not relevant to the murder case against Bill and I have things to do. Please fax me the meeting minutes as soon as they are ready. Sergeant Crombie here will give you the fax number." He turned and walked towards the door."

"No," Dr. Milton replied coldly. "You will receive a copy of the discharge summary which will only be prepared when Bill is actually discharged. That is our procedure. You may leave your contact information with our secretary on the way out." Claire put her head down to cover her smirk and McCoy stomped out of the room without a word, followed by the ever faithful Michael Crombie, who turned to offer the gathering a genial smile before departing.

At the end of the meeting, Bess came over to Marion to give her a copy of her report. "If there is any way I can help further, please let me know. Here is my card." Claire glanced over the card and noted the title, Bess Enright, Ph. D. She recalled that nobody at the meeting had referred to her as doctor and guessed that that was just the way the hospital hierarchy worked. There were the top bananas and then there was everybody else.

Chapter 9—What Will Happen to Bill Now?

Claire and Marion wanted to speak to Ted Ramsey after the meeting ended but he explained that he was going into another meeting shortly and only had a few minutes. Marion told him that Bill was getting more withdrawn every day and if he didn't get settled soon he might never again be the self he had been which was, under his former circumstances, at least somewhat sociable. "Can't you use Bess's report to convince Ms. Watson?" she pleaded.

"It doesn't work that way," Ted replied. "They have to think of their responsibilities to all their clients and they can't afford to take any chances. Privately, I agree with you that it seems unlikely Bill killed that woman but there is no proof."

"Whatever happened to innocent until proven guilty?" Claire asked.

"That is what the courts will decide and that is what the unit manager at the Clive Centre is waiting for. As a matter of fact, she can't wait because they won't be able to keep that bed empty for more than two weeks and the case will never make it to court by then."

"What about another place, then?" pleaded Marion? "Maybe that was not the best place for him anyway. Now with all these community living homes maybe he could go live with two or three others like him and be happier. At Forbes he only really was comfortable with the people who sat at his table because they are the ones he got used to. Maybe that could happen again in a smaller setting?"

Ted's reply was somewhat condescending. "First of all, I don't know what you mean by "others like him." It doesn't make a lot of sense to cluster people with autism together. You can almost guarantee that they will never form a relationship with each other because none of them will ever initiate it." Secondly, PDD is in a funding squeeze and cannot provide more than the most basic financial support to new clients. Hence, existing agencies are unwilling to take on these new clients because it would only mean reducing the quality of life for those individuals they already serve, cutting back on social outings and supervised employment hours, for example....and these have already been reduced."

Marion was looking desperate. She was moaning and clutching at her chest. Claire was concerned and got her to sit down. They had been standing huddled together in the abandoned conference room all this time because of Ted's limited time availability. Ted looked concerned and Claire explained that Marion had a heart condition and that was why she had come to Edmonton to live with her daughter and had brought Bill here so she could still look out for him.

"There is one other possibility," Ted said musingly. It is called 'Family Managed Care' and it is an innovative care provision alternative for those families not willing to let go when their child turns eighteen and place them into a community home outside the family. Usually, it is a transitional phase while families are organizing adult day programs or work placements and seeking out the most compatible permanent care setting for their adult children. That can take a few years but there is no time limit. It is entirely up to the families."

"It makes a lot of sense, especially in this day and age when young adults with perfectly normal functioning are remaining in the family home until their mid-twenties and in some cases even later. Some families contract with agencies to organize staffing and other administrative details but others prefer to do it all themselves with support from PDD to organize some of the administrative issues. But PDD would not fund full staffing coverage right now because of the funding shortfall and they would never pay 24/7 coverage for one person alone in any case."

"Are there other parents out there we could meet up with who might be looking to start something like this and need an extra person to come in?" Claire asked, hopefully.

"There probably are but PDD is not going to give you their names for confidentiality reasons. You could maybe advertise in their newsletter or on their website but that will take time. Also, my experience with parents who want to do it on their own is that they are particularly protective so it does not seem likely that they are going to be too ready to link up with somebody who still has a murder charge hanging over him."

Marion looked dejected again although some color had returned to her face now that she was sitting down. Claire, however, was looking calculating and if McCoy had been there to see that look he would probably have quailed. "How does one get in contact with PDD?" she asked. "I have only ever dealt with Children's Services because of my daughter."

Ted rattled off the number and added, "That is the reception number. You just explain to whoever answers what you want and then you will be forwarded to a specialized intake worker. They close at four so it is probably too late to reach them today. I have to go now but if you have any further questions I will be back in the office Tuesday. I am taking Monday off."

Claire and Marion thanked him and left. "Hmmm," Marion fumed, once Ted was out of earshot. "Nice for him! He can just take off and forget all about Bill. Just put him on the shelf until Tuesday. But God knows what state Bill will be by then."

Claire responded, "Well, he certainly does not have Bess's fire and imagination. Still, I imagine he started out caring. Most social workers do. But in order to survive, given all the grief they see every day, they have to develop a bit of a shell and keep themselves distanced. Those who don't—sooner or later they just burn out. I have known a couple."

"Speaking of burning out," Marion said, "there is something I have been worrying about for a while. Bill's guardianship application is overdue and I have to deal with it. My daughter has never been interested in taking that on with me. And with my heart condition anything could happen. I need to make sure Bill has a co-guardian just in case."

Marion looked meaningfully at Claire but Claire did not respond. She could just imagine what her husband, Dan, would have to say if she agreed to something like that without consulting him first. Finally, she said weakly, "I think that is a good idea."

Claire arrived home to find Jessie's supper dishes in the sink and the kitchen counter cluttered. It was six o'clock and the assistant had left after feeding Jessie, telling Dan she had an assignment to finish for class the next day. She really should have cleaned up before leaving, though. Wearily, Claire set about organizing the kitchen and getting supper ready for her and Dan. Jessie was in her special armchair with the vibrating pad on and her feet stretched out on the footrest, listening to music. Claire heated up some left over lasagna, quickly threw together a salad and in 10 minutes they were eating. They did not stretch this process out because both knew it was only a matter of minutes before Jessie would require attention. When they finished, Dan took Jessie to her commode and Claire cleaned up the kitchen. Then they all settled down in front of the TV but as quickly as they turned it on, Claire turned it off. "I've just got to tell you what happened today," she said and related the case conference outcome, what the social worker had said and Marion's concern about getting a co-guardian.

At this last statement Dan's antennae went up. "I hope you did not volunteer, Claire!"

"No. I wanted to talk to you first. But the fact is I do know a lot about the system."

"It is not about what you know but about all that you would have to do if something happened to Marion—and you did tell me that she has a heart condition. Don't we have enough on our plate with Jessie?"

"I suppose so, but she really does need help. Frankly, I don't know how she would have managed without my help this week."

"Maybe so, but I don't know how much expertise you have with somebody like this Bill guy anyway. It does not sound like he is anything like Jessie. Isn't autism a little out of your league?"

Claire said nothing but just nodded dejectedly. Soon it was time to give Jessie her evening snack and epilepsy medication. Then Claire placed Jessie back on her commode, washed her face, brushed her teeth and put her to bed.

Chapter 10—Jimmy Steps Up

Claire awoke sluggishly the next morning after a restless night of unpleasant dreams about the future for Marion and Bill. She wandered into the kitchen in her pajamas and sat down at the table with a cup of rather stale coffee. It had been made an hour ago by Dan, who had left her sleeping while he got Jessie ready for school and sent her off. Dan had a home office out of which he was able to do most of the computerized engineering work for his company. This happy arrangement made it possible for Dan and Claire to share the work of raising Jessie and meeting all her needs. Once again, Claire marveled at how others in their situation managed—those who had to rush out the door to work every morning, and those who struggled just to get by without any leftover time, money or energy for meeting all the complicated needs that went with Jessie's profound level of disability. She shook her head and picked up the phone. Claire had just had one of her ideas and, as was her nature, she wanted validation and resolution for it immediately!

"Elves here," Jimmy responded gruffly when he answered his cell.

"Jimmy, it's Claire Burke. I thought you would like an update on what is happening to Bill."

"Yeah, sure, but I am on a job right now and kind of busy."

"Can I maybe meet you for lunch? I'd really like to talk to you about the situation."

"I have my lunch with me, and I want to finish this job today so I basically have to work right through."

"Oh, I see," Claire responded, the disappointment evident in her voice.

Jimmy had been caught up in his work and only belatedly remembered how much he owed to Claire—his freedom, since without her it was very unlikely that he would have been cleared from suspicion of murdering his wife. "I am at Las Palmas Restaurant. Somebody sabotaged their outdoor lighting system. It's not far from you. If you can meet me there at 12:30, I can spare half an hour. Will that do? Otherwise, I can see you later on this evening. I should be through here by eight."

"I know where it is. I've been there a few times. I will see you at 12:30," Claire responded gratefully.

Jimmy was just climbing down from a ladder when Claire arrived. He pointed her to a table and excused himself to wash his hands. After opening their respective lunches, ordering something to drink and exchanging a few pleasantries, Claire updated Jimmy on what had been happening to Bill. He was shocked and reiterated what all the others who knew Bill had already said. "I have never seen him be violent except for striking out defensively once when he felt backed into a corner. He never really hurt that nurse—gave him a couple of bruises maybe. It is too bad McCoy had to be the one to get involved. That can only make things worse." Jimmy remembered bitterly how McCoy had been ready to build an entire case around him for his wife's murder without looking any further. It looked like the same thing could happen to Bill. "What can I do to help?" Jimmy asked. "I don't want Bill to go through what I did."

"There's no way to help with the investigation right now, but there are two things you could consider. First, can you possibly bring Mavis up here for a visit so Bill can see her? I think that could help him to get better oriented. He is really confused and upset right now and withdrawing from everybody."

Jimmy looked sad and thoughtful when Claire mentioned Mavis. "I am booked to fly down to Calgary and visit Mavis this Saturday. I really want to move her up here but I haven't figured out how to do it yet. I know Tia once offered to help but she couldn't work 24/7, even if she *is* still willing, and she has to work around her son's schedule which is not the same as my work schedule. Even to bring Mavis up here could be tricky. I suppose if we fly up it won't be too bad. It's a short trip but there is still the wait at the airport. And then what do I do when I get here? She will need personal attention for sure at that point and my parents never wanted my help with her toileting needs. I will have to look after her that way, I suppose, but it's going to be very awkward." Claire knew the story—how patiently Jimmy's parents had worked with Mavis to develop what abilities they could despite her profound physical disabilities, severely limited understanding and lack of any formal communication system. She had been toilet trained but the constant lifting finally got too much for them in those days before ceiling lifts, and they had reluctantly placed her at the Forbes Centre when she was 14. The staff meant well there but they were limited in terms of both their numbers and their understanding of what was possible. Mavis had been placed in diapers and that was how she had lived for the past twenty years.

"I would go with you this Saturday, Jimmy, but Jessie's wonderful assistant has begged off again. No, I misspoke," Claire said bitterly. "Amy just tells me; she never begs or apologizes. It really is 'all about her,' as the saying goes. But why don't you ask Tia? If her parents won't take her son for the weekend, I will." Tia's son, Mario, had just turned nine and Claire enjoyed her relationship with this serious and highly verbal child very much. She was 'Aunty Claire' to him and the feeling of relationship was mutual on her part.

"I could ask her, I guess," Jimmy said with a slight wistfulness in his voice. Then he added, gruffly, to cover his feelings, "I haven't seen her for a while and my house is showing it."

"I thought you had a regular arrangement for her to clean for you?"

"Well, it is kind of informal and I've just let it slide recently. I've been busy." The truth was that Jimmy was finding it more and more disconcerting to be around Tia and he had no idea how she felt about him. He had good reason not to trust women after his late wife's behavior so it had just seemed less painful and awkward to keep his distance until he could get his feelings under control and regain a proper professional relationship towards her.

Claire listened and observed carefully and got the picture but she did not comment on it. Instead she said, "I'll call her if you like. I need to tell her what's happening to Bill, anyway."

After a pause, Jimmy agreed. "Maybe if Tia is willing to come, the best thing would be to just drive down. That way if we need to attend to Mavis' bathroom needs on the way we can just stop. Plane bathrooms would be impossible."

"I think you are right," Claire said soberly. "I will call her, then." Jimmy started to rise and Claire added hastily, "I know you are anxious to get back to work, Jimmy, but there is a second issue. I will try to be quick."

Jimmy sneaked a furtive peek at his watch and then sat down again, reluctantly.

"I am really worried about Marion. She is looking bad with all the stress she has been under. Did you know that she has a pretty serious heart condition?" Jimmy nodded. "She mentioned co-guardianship on the way home from the hospital yesterday. I can't take that on. Dan won't agree because he says Jessie is enough to cope with." Claire paused a moment to gather her courage. "I was wondering if you would consider being Bill's co-guardian since you know him so well and he feels so attached to Mavis?"

"But I already am Bill's co-guardian. Didn't Marion tell you?"

Claire looked dumbfounded. "No. She just said something about guardianship papers and about needing a co-guardian and I thought...."

Jimmy interrupted. "She was probably talking about the renewal. I guess it has been five years since we set up the co-guardianship—although I think the government is now changing it for people like Mavis and Bill. If a doctor or psychologist states that their level of disability is permanent and of such a degree that they will never be capable of managing their own affairs then, once this round of renewals is done, we won't have to do it again."

Claire was only half listening. She was still absorbing the fact that Jimmy had committed to a legal guardianship responsibility towards Bill and relishing the wave of relief washing over her. She hadn't realized how nervous she had been feeling about this issue. "Why did Marion ask you to be Bill's co-guardian?" she asked. "And why did you agree?"

"Ever since my parents died, and that was more than ten years ago—they died six months apart—Marion has kept an eye out for Mavis and reported to me on how she was doing. I couldn't have had Mavis here even for a visit because of my wife's attitude. She could not see anything positive in people with disabilities and wanted nothing to do with Mavis. It seemed better just to leave Mavis there at Forbes—and I was only able to do that without worrying all the time because Marion always watched over her and asked about her when she visited Bill, and kept me informed, but now…." Jimmy trailed off with a worried look on his face. Then he shrugged his shoulders and added, "When Marion asked me, I could hardly say no, and did she tell you what her daughter, Hilda's, attitude is? She sounds the same as my late wife."

"Are you going to renew the co-guardianship?" Claire asked.

"Yes," Jimmy said thoughtfully. "I can do that much for her. It doesn't sound like she is functioning too efficiently these days so I better help with the process. I had to renew Mavis' guardianship last year so my criminal record check is still valid. What we need is a new capacity assessment on Bill and that could be tricky because he does not have a doctor here who knows him."

"Would a recent psychological assessment do?"

"That would be even better," Jimmy said.

"I'll ask Bess. She just did a very thorough assessment of both intellectual and personality functioning."

"Great! Then we should be able to get this process out of the way very quickly. When will you be able to ask her?"

"I am going up there today—and I will also call Tia about this weekend and see if she can work it out. I will get back to you as soon as I know."

They both rose and said their good-byes. Claire left with a sense of lightness. At least something had been accomplished. She checked her watch. It was 1:30. She had taken an extra ½ hour of Jimmy's time but it was so worth it. Now what? Amy was supposed to be at the house at 3:40 to meet the school bus when Jessie arrived so she did not have to worry about her daughter. In any case, Dan was working at home. Claire headed to the hospital to check on the situation and update Marion. She also wanted to talk to Bess if by any chance she was around.

Chapter 11—a New Source of Support for Bill

The receptionist at the desk in Bill's unit told Claire that Bess was no longer on the unit but somewhere else in the hospital. When asked for her cell phone number Claire got the predictable response. "I'm sorry. We can't give out that information." Claire turned away, frustrated. But just then Bess walked through the door and headed straight to the reception desk.

"I forgot to drop this report off when I was here earlier," she said. "Could you see that Dr. Milton gets it, please?" The receptionist took the report with an affirmative nod just as Claire tapped Bess on the shoulder. She whirled around, startled, and then greeted Claire with a big smile. "Hi, I didn't see you there. I tend to get overly focused at times. Bill is holding his own but not happy. Marion was still with him when I left an hour ago. She might be there now."

"It's you I want to talk to, Bess. Can we have a word in private, please? It won't take long."

"Okay," Bess said slowly, "but I'm due at a case conference in 15 minutes."

"I'll be quick," Claire said. The receptionist was looking on curiously.

"Let's see if we can find an empty interview room."

"Try Two," the receptionist interjected.

Claire entered the room after Bess and closed the door. She hurriedly expressed her concerns about Marion and the need to expedite the renewal of the co-guardianship. "We need to get a capacity assessment done. Could you do it? Have you done them before?"

"Lots," Bess replied, and I already have a spare form. I can write it up quickly from my report and refer the court officials back to my full report, if they want further information. I can have it ready for you tomorrow."

"Wonderful!" Claire exclaimed. "Oh, can I ask what your fee will be?" she said nervously.

"Nada—but don't mention it at the front desk. I want to see Bill get the help he needs. Are you the co-guardian?"

"No-o-o," Claire admitted, sensing a problem. "It's a friend of Marion's—the brother of the Mae-Mae person he's always referring to."

"Well, I really should get the request from Marion then."

"Trust me, she will be delighted that you are willing to do it. We could go to Bill's room now and see if she is still there."

"I have no time. Have to run. Don't worry. I'll do it tonight anyway and get her approval tomorrow. I have seen how she relies on you." And with that Bess was off before Claire could even say a proper thank you.

When Claire returned to the reception desk, the unit clerk told her that Bill was having an afternoon nap and Marion had asked to use one of the empty interview rooms to meet with someone. Claire found her talking earnestly to a stranger.

"Claire! I'm so glad you are here. This is the lawyer you mentioned who would be coming—Jack Anders. Jack, this is Claire Burke. She's the person I told you about who has been helping me so much with all this."

"I'm happy to meet you, Claire. Marion tells me you have been a wonderful support for her. We have just been going through the case against Bill and perhaps you can clarify a couple of points for me that Marion was not quite sure about. Can you tell me exactly what you saw when you entered Bill's room at Clive Centre after the murder?"

"I can do better than that!" Claire said, and whipped out her cell phone. A half hour later, Claire had reviewed every minute of that fateful meeting. She was also able to relate the key points of the psychology and occupational therapy assessments, including Bill's non-history of violence and his weak right hand strength. She carefully did not mention anything about the guardianship, though. Claire had a nervous feeling that if he knew the previous order had expired, Marion might lose control of Bill's care.

Jack listened carefully to all of this and when Claire finished talking, he asked, "Can I get a copy of that psychology report?"

"Bess gave me a copy at the meeting. I have it at my daughter's home," Marion replied. I know Hilda has a fax machine and I will get her to send it to you. What is your fax number?"

"That's great!" Jack replied. "I'm sure the crown prosecutor will subpoena one later but this will give me a head start." Jack paused for a moment and then went on. "The evidence against Bill seems questionable thanks to your quick thinking in taking those pictures, Claire, and the assessment results on the left-right difference and all the anecdotal information to the effect that he has always been strongly left handed. I would like to get some blow ups of your cell phone pictures though, so I can examine the blood spatter pattern on Bill's hands. Can you send them to my cell and I will take care of that. Here is my number," he said, handing her his card.

"When will it get to court?" Marion asked nervously.

"Well, the preliminary hearing will probably happen in a week or two but there is enough evidence, ambiguous as it is, to likely get it bound over for trial.

The actual trial date will likely be months from now, though, dependent on the court docket. They are usually backed up but they may give priority to a case like this. I don't know."

"That's just the problem," Claire responded. "Bill is going to be kept here until the case is settled and I just know he's not going to hold out. He's very agitated and it's a matter of time before he lashes out and then that will go against him in court."

"And I can't stand to see him so unhappy," Marion moaned.

"I'll work on that one," Jack assured her. "But do you have an alternate placement for him if I can get the prosecutor's office to agree that he can leave?"

"According to the Social Worker here, that is unlikely," Claire replied. "He doesn't think any community living home will take him until his name is cleared and the Clive Centre has definitely said they won't take him back. Within two weeks they will be giving his room to the next person on their wait list if he's not cleared by that time."

"Have you explored other options?"

"I'm thinking," Claire said tersely.

"Well, I'll get back to you as soon as I know something." And with that, the lawyer rose and left the room.

Claire could see that Marion was relieved by this new source of support and they spent some minutes speculating about what Jack Anders might be able to do to get Bill released from the hospital and to ultimately clear his name.

"By the way," Claire said, "I talked to Jimmy today and he said he's already Bill's co-guardian!" Then Claire told her about the arrangements she'd made with Jimmy and Bess.

"That's wonderful news!" Marion exclaimed. "I had almost forgotten that Jimmy had signed on as co-guardian and it's great that he's willing to continue in that role even after what has happened. I'll see Bess tomorrow and assure her about the assessment. But then I'll need a lawyer to do the court work. Maybe Jack can handle it!"

"You said it was overdue already," Claire responded. "Is it wise to even let him know? He might say you have no legal authority now and he can't deal with you about Bill anymore."

"I know other parents and family members at Forbes who let their orders expire and nothing happened to them. But maybe I can call CARP. I know they help people with completing guardianship orders and they have their own volunteer lawyers. There must be an Edmonton branch. I'll look it up in the phone book when I get back to Hilda's place."

"What's CARP?"

"I think it stands for Canadian Association for Retired Persons. It's the main advocacy group for seniors across the country and there are lots of local chapters. They also help people with disabilities on will and guardianship matters."

Claire pulled out her cell and opened the internet. In a minute she had the contact information and wrote it down for Marion. "If you can take care of the guardianship issue, I will focus on another matter." Claire told her about the plan to get Mavis up to Edmonton for a visit that weekend.

Marion was predictably very pleased but understood the concerns. "Pick up a container of baby wipes and send along some extra plastic bags and disposable paper change pads—and diapers, of course—in case you need to change her along the way."

"I have some already," Claire said. "Jessie's old wheelchair has a built-in commode unit but no lift, so we always had to find a place to lay her down to undress her when she needed to go the bathroom when we were travelling. What fun that was! I almost dropped her a few times and on one occasion I thought I had broken my back."

"What do you mean—'her old chair'?"

"Oh, her new chair has a built-in lift," Claire said airily. "I guess you didn't notice when she was up here the other day."

"That's amazing! How…"[ii]

"Another time," Claire said. "I've got to run now. I need to talk to Tia and see if she can help out with bringing Mavis up."

Chapter 12—Amy is Finally Helpful

Tia was at home waiting for her nine year old son, Mario, to get back from school when Claire got there. She greeted Claire warmly, looking forward to a nice visit with her best friend. Once they settled down at the kitchen table with a cup of coffee and a piece of the apple cake Tia was known for, Claire began. She told Tia all that had happened and was happening to Bill, how he was responding and the toll the whole process was taking on Marion. Tia was predictably appalled. "Are you quite sure he did not kill that nurse?"

"Anything is possible, I guess, but it does not fit with his personality as we know it. If they had had an altercation that night which upset him enough to lash out at her, the other staff would have heard something. And even if he had been upset he would have struck out at her directly, not by stabbing her in the back."

"Is there anything I can do to help?" Tia asked.

Claire had been waiting for an opening like this and she mentioned the plan to get Mavis up for a visit that weekend. "Could you travel down there with Jimmy on Saturday and help him bring Mavis back? I can't do it myself because I have no help for Jessie this weekend. Amy is going skiing in Jasper apparently." Claire explained with a tone of exasperation in her voice.

"She's always letting you down. Are you going to do something about that?"

"It's on my list," Claire replied laconically. "Well, what about this weekend?"

"I don't know. My parents would take Mario so that's not a problem, but I haven't seen Jimmy in months and it would be very awkward."

"He's okay with it. He said he's been very busy of late and that's why he hasn't called you to do more cleaning."

Tia still hesitated. "It would be really awkward for me travelling all that way with him alone. I'm trying to keep up a professional relationship."

"Well, maybe you shouldn't try so hard," Claire said with a smile. She knew exactly what was bothering Tia but did not say it out loud. "I can't go and Marion has to stay with Bill, and her daughter would not even think of it so if you won't go there's nobody else to ask. Bill is in a really bad state. Don't you want to help him?"

After some further hesitation, Tia asked, "What if she has a bowel accident in the car? How could I clean her up and change her?"

"I'll give you everything you need to get there and the Forbes Center will likely provide you with some supplies, too." Tia finally agreed but she did not look happy about it.

On Thursday evening, Claire was sitting at her desk going through unpaid invoices and wishing there were more of them, more clients to invoice that is, when the phone rang.

"Hello, Claire. It's Amy. My mom just reminded me that I should call and let you know my ski trip got cancelled so I guess I can work Saturday after all."

Claire sat stunned for a moment, trying to figure out how to respond. It had occurred to her that having Bill and Tia obliged to make the trip together was a good thing. Finally, she said weakly, "Oh, that's good, Amy! I'll see you Saturday, then." Claire hung up the phone and sat a few minutes contemplating what to do next. She really needed to let Tia know. Their friendship was very important to Claire and she knew Tia hated trickery in any form. She would not easily forgive Claire for duping her into making this trip with Jimmy unnecessarily. Regretfully, she picked up the phone. Tia's son, Mario, answered it.

"Hello, Mario. Is your mom there?"

"She's in the shower, Aunty Claire. Do you want me to ask her to call you?"

"Okay. I just wanted to tell her that she won't have to go to Calgary this weekend. Jessie's helper just called and said she can come in Saturday after all."

There was an uncharacteristic silence on the other end of the line, uncharacteristic because Mario was usually so quick on the uptake. Finally, Mario spoke. "Aunty Claire," he said thoughtfully. "*Please* don't tell mom."

"Why?"

"You *know* why," he said pleadingly.

Claire thought for a moment but then said, in a conspiring voice, "Okay...just tell her the phone call was a wrong number—and act normal. Your mother is no fool!"

"Okay," he whispered, and as he was hanging up the phone, Claire heard a slight giggle. She just hoped he was as capable of being sneaky as she had become over the last year!

Chapter 13—Claire Has an Idea

It was Saturday morning and Claire was being punished for her sneakiness, something she had almost come to expect. Amy had not turned up at eight that morning as arranged and, when Claire called, Amy said she was not feeling well but would come in at eleven after a couple of hours more sleep. She talked as if she was doing Claire a favor by this but to Claire's ears Amy sounded hung over rather than sick. But whatever the reason was, this left Claire to feed Jessie her breakfast and to brush her teeth. Claire liked to multi-task so as she fed Jessie her specially prepared and ground high fiber cereal with pureed prunes added, she was at the same time trying to drink her coffee and glance through the newspaper. Some days it was a long and tedious process to feed Jessie and this was one of those days. Jessie was coughing a lot, a sign she was aspirating bits of food, so Claire had to proceed very slowly and carefully and wait between 'bites.' These were not really bites as such since all of Jessie's food had to be finely pureed. Claire was not good at waiting. In fact, nobody would say that patience was one of her virtues—hence the multi-tasking. As she sat there thinking of the new client appointments she had set up for this Saturday and then had to cancel, and how it had been too late to rebook them once Amy finally got around to calling her, Claire felt more and more angry and decided that this time she was really going to do something about it.

When Jessie finally finished eating and drinking enough—and drinking was an even bigger problem than eating—Dan took her to the bathroom. Claire moved her coffee and paper to the table beside her favorite armchair and settled herself in it for a few minutes of peace and quiet. She could hear Dan filling the raised jet tub and knew that he would sit with Jessie while she was in it. Jessie enjoyed the feel of the water bubbling against her skin very much so she should be good for half an hour at least. Claire took the sports section of the paper over to Dan and brought a chair near the change and laundry room where the tub was. Then she returned to her paper but after a couple of minutes flicked to the classified ads section. Claire was now determined to get rid of Amy but she needed to find a good replacement first. People willing and able to work with individuals with severe to profound disabilities were always in strong demand so few bothered to waste money advertising and none of the ads in that section met her needs. She would have to advertise, herself. Claire glanced through the help wanted ads in the 'domestic worker wanted' section and suddenly her eyes froze on one of them, an advertisement for housekeeping assistance at the Clive Centre. "Tia could do it," she mused—"and I could get the bus to drop Mario off here after school and help him with his homework. She could gradually start talking with the other housekeeping persons and maybe learn something about who could have done the murder." Excitedly, she walked over to tell Dan and Jessie about her great idea.

Dan's response was less than encouraging, however. "So as we speak, Tia is driving to Calgary with Jimmy, something she did not want to do, due to your earlier maneuvering. And now you want to orchestrate her weekdays as well, knowing how sensitive she is around the issue of being perceived as a cleaning lady!"

"But we are at a dead end," Claire exclaimed. McCoy is convinced Bill did the murder and he's not going to bother looking any further. And unless Tia goes in there I have no access. It's not as if I could do it myself. They already know me."

"And we both know you are not that fond of cleaning in any case," Dan added with a sardonic smirk. He went on, "I can understand why you don't trust McCoy to do his job but what about the lawyer? Didn't he say the case was not strong enough to get a conviction?"

"Yes, but that's not the same as finding Bill innocent. It will always be hanging over his head."

"Well, I guess that's one of the few benefits of his condition. Bill won't know the difference."

"Sure, but any community living home operator looking to take him on will know. They always do background checks. And the Clive Centre director has already said that Bill can't come back unless he's completely cleared—and they are giving away his bed in two weeks. So he's going to end up spending the rest of his life in a secure unit in a mental hospital with other people with all kinds of problems. And all the gains he's made in socialization through the years will be lost!"

"Oh, it can't be as bad as all that. Somebody will take him on. And anyway, I don't understand why other people's problems become your problems. Are you bored with your life or something?"

Claire ignored this last rejoinder and returned to the previous point. "Let's just say that you were running a home for two vulnerable people and looking for a third. If you did not know anything about Bill except that he had been suspected of murdering a staff member would you take him on?" she asked rhetorically.

"Well, I guess we'll just have to wait and see what happens."

"Yeah—and by that time he'll be such a basket case that *nobody* will want him. You can't just put people with autism on ice, you know. We have to find a solution and there's not much time to do it. He's withdrawing more every day and reverting to all the autistic self-stimulatory behaviors he used to have when he was younger."

"Okay, but you are still wrong about one thing. It's not our problem. It's Marion's problem."

"You haven't even met her or you would see how frail she is looking—and I just found out that Bill's guardianship order has lapsed. She's busy working on that. Also, she's new to Edmonton. She does not have the time, the energy or the resources to help Bill."

Dan was about to respond but Jessie interjected, making it clear that it was time for her to get out of the tub and get on with her day. Dan turned the jets off and Claire took over bathing Jessie and washing her hair while the tub drained. Then she rinsed her well with the telephone shower while Dan laid out one of her thick bath towels on the change table and then maneuvered her back into the sling for the transfer. Claire went off to get some clothes for Jessie for the day while Dan began drying her. Claire dried and shaped Jessie's hair which had a little natural curl and always looked very nice if simply dried in the right shape. Claire wished she had the same hair but that was another issue. Once Jessie was back in her chair, Claire brushed her teeth and then Dan took her over to her easy chair and lifted her into it, turning on the massage pad already there. Claire felt a guilty twinge about not doing the exercises but Jessie looked happy so Claire sat down on the neighboring sofa and read the newspaper to her. Jessie did not understand but she always enjoyed people talking to her or reading to her. Claire worked her way through the crossword puzzle after she saw that Jessie was dozing off and then she got her lunch ready and Amy arrived to take over. As Claire sat in her office going through her receipts once more she wondered idly how Tia was doing but was sure she was managing. They were probably in Calgary by now.

Chapter 14—A Fateful Trip

Jimmy picked Tia and Mario up at 8:30 in the morning and they drove to Tia's parents in Wetaskiwin, 20 miles south of Edmonton. Tia's father, Alberto, had managed to retire a few years earlier and had taken up landscape painting because he'd been so struck by the wonderful natural light in Alberta. He was touching up his latest painting and Mario was eager to see it. Tia's mother, Marisa, was sitting companionably nearby reading an Inspector Brunetti mystery. After introducing Jimmy to them, and after Jimmy had commented favorably on Alberto's painting, they said good-bye to Mario and Tia issued some final admonishments to him. Once they were back on the road, Tia allowed herself the luxury of really looking at Jimmy. "You've lost weight!" she blurted.

"It's been very busy at work. We're doing the electrical installation for the new 28-story apartment building going up downtown where the old Gold Rush Hotel used to be. I have also had a lot of fussy details to settle over my late wife's affairs."

Tia chose to respond to the former statement. "I've seen the apartment layouts for that new building advertised in the paper. The interiors are in Art Deco style," she said, quietly grateful for this factoid she had picked up from her son. I understand that they are being sold as Condos and some of them are quite large. I certainly would not mind living there."

"I thought you liked gardening?"

"I do but keeping a house up on my own is no treat. I would prefer less work and less worry."

"Well, Mario would miss it, I bet."

"At first he might but he's very resourceful—and it takes him about a minute to make new friends!" She could not keep a small note of pride out of her voice and Jimmy smiled slightly.

"Good for him. I certainly could not make friends easily when I was his age. I guess I was a little on the shy side."

"Well, I was a little on the alienated side after listening to all my parent's early negative remarks about "the English," and having a few negative experiences myself because of being Italian. By the time they finally adjusted to living in a new country and were able to see most of the Canadians they knew as just people like themselves, it was too late for me and I guess I'm still a little on the prickly side."

Jimmy smiled openly. "If you say so but whatever it is, I kind of like it."

Tia laughed. "Well, we're a fine pair, aren't we?" Too late she realized what she had said and turned her head towards the window so he would not see her blushing. Tia searched desperately for ways to keep the conversation going without letting it become too personal. Beside her, Jimmy was having the same struggle and he reached over to turn the radio on. In the process, his arm touched hers and she jumped involuntarily. That did it for Jimmy. He slowed the car and turned the right hand signal on. They were approaching the turn-off for Pigeon Lake Provincial Park and he took it.

"Where are we going?" Tia asked.

"I'll show you when we get there," he responded tersely.

They drove another five minutes down the road and Jimmy pulled into a little roadside parking area where some picnic benches were laid out and the trees surrounding the little enclosure formed a pleasant umbrella. He turned to her fiercely. "You want to know why I really lost weight? It's all the lonely nights and all the energy I've spent avoiding you. I love you, you see. I have loved you practically from the day I met you. And I would love nothing more than to be a father to your funny son. I think he's the neatest, sweetest kid I have ever met. And I can't drive all the way to Calgary with you, pretending I don't care and talking about Condos and other trivia. So if that makes you uncomfortable I'll turn around and drive you home now. I can manage on my own with my sister. Don't you worry about *that*. But I refuse to pretend any longer," he ended lamely.

Tia sat stunned and said nothing for a moment. Then she leaned over and shyly leaned her head on his chest. She felt like a great cleansing flood was washing over her and all the anger and hurt of years was being driven away by its power. "I love you, too," she muttered indistinctly, her face now firmly wedged against his chest.

"What?" he asked.

Tia said nothing. Maybe she had misheard or misunderstood. She had dreamed about this for so long that maybe she was hallucinating.

Jimmy lifted her face up so he could look her in the eyes. "Repeat what you said," he ordered. Whatever it is I can take it."

Tia looked at him fearfully. Was this really happening? Was she about to make a fool of herself? "I love you, too," she whispered.

Jimmy groaned in relief. "Say it again," he said. "I want to make sure I heard you right."

"I love you," she said, a little louder. "I have loved you for a very long time. And I want to look after you and to take away the hurt I still see in your eyes."

"No, I want to look after *you*—and that son of yours. I only hope he will let me be a father to him—and we can go to art galleries together and do other stuff. I know you don't like art galleries but I hear that Mario does," he said.

Jimmy was referring back to an incident which had happened shortly before he had met Tia and shortly after the murder of his late wife. He had heard the story much later, how Tia had eagerly and gratefully agreed to clean Claire's house and how Claire had just as eagerly agreed to take Mario to a show at the art gallery and how both of them had thought that they were getting a great deal and the other one was a fool to make such a trade! Tia responded, "I don't hate art galleries or art. I'm not as artistic as your late wife apparently was but I do have some aesthetic sensibility. I just hate driving in traffic and parking and going to new places. It kind of intimidates me!"

"Well, lucky for you I like driving," Jimmy chuckled. "And I'm going to be around to prevent anything or anybody from intimidating you anymore. "If you ever have to deal with McCoy or anybody like him again, just watch me!"

Tia saw the macho pride that had suddenly appeared in his eyes and in the lift of his shoulders, and felt the new energy that appeared to be emanating from him. She felt sad for all the years he had been half crushed by his late wife, who, reportedly, had been a cold, selfish and uncaring person. Tia wrapped her arms around him and he wrapped his around her. He did not try to kiss her. He did not even want to at this moment. He was too overwhelmed with all his feelings. They sat there like that for several minutes and all Jimmy said out loud was a prayer. "Praise you, Jesus. Thank you, Jesus. All glory and honor is yours, almighty Father, now and forever. Amen."

Tia looked up in surprise but the words felt right. It was like they had both been struggling separately through a vast desert and had finally come out on the other side. Someone must have led them there. Finally they pulled apart and leaned back against the seats, emotionally exhausted. After a couple more minutes, Tia reached over and pulled his head to her breast. She kissed him gently on the cheek and he allowed himself to nestle there for a couple of minutes, feeling like he had finally come home. Then he pulled away and shook himself. "We've got to go—if only I can remember how to drive!" They returned to the highway and wheeled away, each wrapped up in their own thoughts. This time there was no need for words or music and the silence was a welcome balm lapping over them and reminding them of all their future possibilities together.

Chapter 15—Reality Intrudes

Tia and Jimmy were just passing Red Deer, half-way to Calgary, when Tia spoke again. "When can we be married?" Being a conventional Catholic girl, alternatives had not even occurred to her.

"Tomorrow would suit me fine," Jimmy responded.

Tia could now afford to let her practical side kick in. "Well, that is obviously not possible, the need to get a license and all. But I don't want any fuss. I had that the first time around and look what it got me. I would be happy to just go away somewhere, do the deed and come back and have a party for our friends.

"Suits me," Jimmy said. "But in church, I hope."

"Well, that is a problem, isn't it? Since I was married before in the church and am therefore in the eyes of God still married."

"Maybe you could get an annulment. He left *you,* after all."

"That is a big time and money-consuming process and in the end I think it's a farce. It reminds me of the ancient Egyptians paying to ensure their souls would be transported to heaven. Besides, I'm not sure if God made up that rule or some early church patriarchs did. And I don't like following other people's rules very much."

"Maybe someday circumstances will change and then we can be remarried in the church."

"Yeah, but we would probably have to renounce our years together and admit we had been living in a state of sin and ask forgiveness. I would not be able to regret the years I had spent with you at that point so it would all be a lie."

"Well, what about the Eucharist? We won't be able to partake because we won't be in a state of grace."

"I feel very much in a state of grace right now and no sexist priest is going to tell me otherwise. Besides, I imagine Mario and I will be moving to your house so that means a different church where I am not known. And you are just a poor widower so you're good to go."

Jimmy grinned broadly. Obviously, he had his hands full! "How about if we doctor our records and run off to Hawaii and get some priest who doesn't know us to give us a wedding mass in his church?" he asked, half humorously.

"Since God presumably also keeps an eye on what happens in Hawaii that would defeat the purpose!" Tia responded lightly. Then, in a more serious vein, she said, "I am not that callous or disrespectful of Catholicism. We will have to get married in a registry office. I just don't want to do it here."

"What will your parents say? What about your son? You once mentioned to me that he took his first communion last year. He will know this goes against the church's teachings. Aren't you afraid of undermining his faith?"

"First of all, my parents love me and they have been very sad and distressed over my situation. They will just be very relieved and pleased that I finally have someone I can rely on and someone who will be a real father to their grandson, on whom they dote. Secondly, Mario is already asking questions about the church and is not prepared to accept blind dogma. He also is going to be very happy for me because in his little boy way he, too, worries about my happiness!"

"I can't remember when in my life I have ever felt happier," Jimmy interjected, and they let the conversation slide for a while as they moved further down the road.

An hour later, Jimmy raised the topic again. "You know I would like you to at least check into this notion of an annulment without dismissing it out of hand. In my mind this is a holy union we are proposing which has more right than many to be blessed by God and I would be grateful if you would at least look into it. I happen to know somebody who went through the process and had a similar story to yours and it was all over in a matter of a few months."

"Okay, I will talk to my priest. He has always felt badly for what happened to me so perhaps he would try to expedite it."

"Good. Now there is something else I would like to ask you about. You said you did not want to get married here. Among Megan's papers I found the deed to a property she apparently bought outright in Mexico. It's near Playa del Carmen, south of Cancun. From the photos it looks like it's near a beach. I don't know with what money she bought it, maybe drug money, and I don't care after all that I have been through. But sooner or later I have to go down there to arrange with some property manager to rent it out, either on a long-term or a week to week basis. Would you consider getting married in Mexico, in one of their beautiful Baroque churches, if that proves to be a possibility—and having our honeymoon there?

"I think that would be very appropriate. It's not as if she ever went there. We might as well try to wring some good out of the bad. Besides, we might as well use what we have instead of wasting money unnecessarily."

What a change that attitude is from Megan's approach to things, Jimmy thought to himself, happily. Then he said, somewhat defensively, "There is one more thing I would like to clear up. It's about Mavis. I want her living in Edmonton as soon as possible. I don't know what arrangements I can make or how fast and she might have to stay with us for a while until I can get her settled. Would you be okay with that?"

"I like your sister—better than a lot of women I know. I only met her once but she seems to me to have a very sweet, trusting personality. And she is not likely to criticize my cooking or make helpful suggestions—so that alone makes her an improvement over lots of sisters-in-law!" Tia added, with a grin.

"People stay sweet like Mavis when they are well loved, I think," Jimmy said quietly. "A lot of my parent's time and attention went into keeping Mavis happy and interested in life."

"The thing is," Tia went on, "I wouldn't know how to look after her, how to meet all her personal needs. I would have to learn, I guess."

"I'm not interested in turning you into Mavis's servant," Jimmy responded gruffly. I would have to hire staff for her. I have already hired staff for this week. Mavis has some money saved up from her monthly AISH allowance. There aren't many ways to spend it when you live in an institution. And Megan left behind some money I can use although I have no idea how she came by it nor do I want to know. If the money runs out I guess we would have to live pretty economically for a while until we can get government support in place. Would you be okay with that?"

"We are not going to pay staff 24/7. We are not the Rockefellers. And I know from Claire's experiences that you can't always count on staff. We are going to have to learn to cope on our own. And even if we do find a place for her we are going to have to have some degree of control over the situation so we can be sure that she is treated appropriately." After a pause, Tia went on, "I have to admit I am bothered by the bowel incontinence issue. I can handle wet diapers but I am not sure about the other. Didn't you say that Mavis was toilet trained at one point?"

"Yes, she had her own special commode with supportive padded straps and a padded seat. I remember also that it was raised at the front a little to keep her from slumping forward. If she did not feel secure she could not function. Some days she could be dry the whole day and others not, but she never had bowel accidents unless she was really sick. The problem is we could not communicate with her directly to find out what she needed so she just had to be taken to the bathroom on a schedule—every two hours, if I remember."

"I know you said that they did not carry that on at the hospital but do you think she could be trained again at this point?"

"I am not sure. Sometimes when I have visited her she gets agitated and starts fussing and then it happens so it is like she is still trying to tell us. It is very sad really. But I don't know if there is any point in trying to start that up again now. We'd have to get a special commode constructed and then it might all be for nothing."

"Well, we're going to try," Tia said firmly. "I'm pretty sure Jessie is more cognitively disabled than Mavis and she's trained. So I don't see why Mavis should hang around in diapers. Claire will know what to do and who to contact for the equipment. She will help me."

Jimmy said nothing but he smiled happily. It was a whole new world for him having a partner to help him work things out.

Chapter 16—Mavis Is Waiting

They drove straight through to Calgary and when they arrived at the Forbes Center, Mavis was ready and waiting for them. "Mavis had a good lunch," the LPN who had been getting her ready said, "and she has a heavy diaper on so she should be good for the trip as long as you go straight through and get going right away. We gave her a suppository early this morning as you suggested so *that* part is taken care of!"

"Great!" Jimmy said, looking sideways at Tia, who in turn, looked embarrassed. "Ah, you should have been at our house when I was growing up," he said. "Mavis's daily bathroom functioning was a favorite topic of conversation at the dinner table!" He grinned at the nurse who, like him, had long since come to terms with the concept that human beings are just glorified animals.

"I don't think the power chair is going to fit into my van, though," Jimmy went on. "We will have to take her old chair. Can you call maintenance to get the seating system out of the power chair once I lift Mavis into the car? We can fold the old chair and put it in the trunk and strap the seating system into one side of the back seat."

"Okay. I will call now," the nurse replied. "And we can lock the power chair up in the storage room until you decide what to do with it. It's not much use to her anyway because she cannot drive it without bashing into things."

"Thanks! Tia, can you wheel the other chair down, please?" Tia was looking at Jimmy, confused.

"People who are as disabled as Jessie and Mavis can't use regular wheelchairs. The back and seat portions have to be specially modified to accommodate their bodies and they need supportive straps and trunk support to keep them safe and comfortable and sitting properly."

Tia nodded. "I guess I knew that because of Jessie. I just never thought about it. It's really a complicated process, isn't it?"

"Yep!" Jimmy replied, laconically. Meanwhile, Mavis was looking from one to the other of them and appeared to be trying to process what was happening. Whatever it was, she seemed to think it was something positive and gurgled happily.

A few minutes later, Tia watched silently as Jimmy lifted Mavis into the front seat of the van. Putting her in the back would have required a lot of stretching and reaching more likely to lead to a back injury. Tia began to appreciate for the first time what it was like to deal with a completely dependent person of adult size. Mavis was not heavy, probably about 120 pounds, Tia guessed, but that was still almost twice the weight of Jessie. Tia's secret, romantic idea that Jimmy and she could manage with Mavis all on their own and, together with Mario, be just be one happy family, began to falter. Her silent judgment against Jimmy's parents for placing Mavis in an institution in the first place began to fade.

Tom, the maintenance man, met them in the parking garage and quickly removed the insert. "Be careful you don't lose any screws. I'd be really stuck then!" Jimmy said. "And thanks for coming so quickly!" Jimmy stored the seating insert in the back seat. Then, they said good-bye to Tom, and left quickly.

After stopping once at a combination garage and convenience store outside Calgary where they gassed up, took turns using the washroom and bought some snacks for the road, they drove straight through. Mavis seemed happy and every once in a while Jimmy reached over and stroked her hand to reassure her. Although the trip back was relatively uneventful, after almost eight hours of driving there and straight back they were exhausted by the time they reached Jimmy's house. He had offered to drop Tia off at her home first but she insisted on staying and helping to get Mavis settled. Mario had chosen to remain with his grandparents for the weekend and Tia's father had offered to bring him directly to school on Monday morning.

Jimmy parked the car in front of the house, unlocked the front door and propped it open. Then he lifted Mavis out of the car and carried her directly in, laying her down on the single bed in his spare bedroom. Tia changed her while Jimmy put the wheelchair back together. When he returned with the reassembled chair, Jimmy said he was going to spend a few minutes massaging and stretching Mavis's legs before he lifted her into it. Once he was beside the bed so Mavis could not roll off, Tia left to wash her hands and stated that she was going to get some supper ready for them. The Forbes' kitchen had provided a meal for Mavis and she just had to microwave it. Later, while Jimmy was eating, Tia insisted on feeding Mavis and managed quite well since she had had some practice with Jessie. Then Jimmy took over to get her to drink enough while Tia ate.

And what was Mavis doing all this time? Unlike Jessie, she could see, and she kept looking around as if trying to figure out where she was. When Jimmy came over to give her her drink, she gurgled happily but she had been patient and comfortable with Tia's tentative efforts at feeding her too. Tia had worried constantly that she would choke Mavis. "It just takes practice," Jimmy assured her.

By eight o'clock, Tia was literally trembling with fatigue. "Could you manage without me now, Jimmy? I'd like to go home."

"Yeah, Mavis seems happy to be here and we'll be fine. I've had lots of practice. Take my car. I'm sorry I can't drive you."

"No. Something might happen and you might need it. I'll call Claire and see if she can pick me up. What time would you like me to come back in the morning to help?"

"No need to help. I've already arranged with an agency to provide support staff from 8 to 4 all week. The rest I can manage myself. But I would like to see you. We have a lot to talk about—and I don't want to leave the support person here alone with Mavis so you would need to come here."

"Okay. I'll call Claire now."

Chapter 17—Girl Talk

In a short while Tia was home and she was sitting with Claire at her kitchen table drinking decaf coffee. "You look exhausted, Tia—but there is also something else, isn't there?" Claire asked.

"How did you know?"

"I know you pretty well."

"Ooh, Claire! Jimmy and I are getting married!"

"I thought as much. Well, I'm glad the plan worked. I was getting sick and tired of the suspense!"

"What plan? You would have gone. You were the logical person to go—if Amy hadn't goofed off!"

"Oh, Amy was with Jessie today, this afternoon, anyway, and in body if not in spirit. I really have to get rid of her!"

"But you said..."

"She phoned me Thursday night to say her ski trip fell through and she could work."

"But why didn't you call? I thought you were my friend!"

"I am your friend—I was doing it for your own good. Besides, it wasn't actually my idea," Claire said defensively. "I *did* call—but you were in the shower....and then I got talked out of telling you."

"Who?"

"Your son."

"My son!?!"

"Yes! When I phoned and told him Amy was available he begged me not to tell you. His thinking was that the two of you could not survive a four hour car ride alone together without one of you cracking."

Tia just looked at Claire and shook her head. "My son?" she repeated.

"You still really don't know who you have there, do you?" Claire said wistfully.

Tia sat silently for a couple of minutes taking it all in. Then she turned to Claire. "Can you call Dan and ask if he can manage with Jessie so you can stay the night? I'm just too wired. I can't stand to be alone."

The two friends talked late into the night about Jimmy, about Mavis, about Bill and Marion. Everything seemed to be happening at once. Tia told Claire about the care provision arrangements that Jimmy had made and what he had said about not becoming a servant to Mavis. Claire applauded him heartily for that, and this gave her the opening she had been looking for. "Actually, Tia, there's something else I want to talk you about. Until Bill is completely cleared, it's unlikely any agency is going to take him on. And if he has to stay in the hospital, which is really taking its toll on him, one of us will have to go trotting back and forth with Mavis all the time just to keep him sane, and that means she will have to stay here permanently, not just for a visit, and that has all kinds of implications in terms of the logistics which will have to be worked out. I don't see how there would be any time for a wedding unless you want to settle for a quick trip to the Registrar's Office."

"Yeah, I know," Tia sighed. "I keep trying to convince myself that it has nothing to do with me and that Mavis is fine without him; he's the one hung up on her. But it isn't working. I keep thinking of Marion and it just does not feel very good. But I don't know what we can do, anyway."

"I do" Claire replied.

"What?"

"I really do want to get rid of Amy, so I was looking at want ads in the classified section today to find out how to word mine. I came across an ad for a part-time housekeeper at the Clive Centre on the same floor where Bill was. If you took that position you could snoop around and talk to people. I just know that something is going on there we have not heard about."

"How is it you are always finding cleaning jobs for me? You will recall that the last one you set up almost got me killed!"

"Well, I would do it myself but they've met me."

"Not to mention that you hate housework and are not much good at it anyway and have no relevant employment references so they would not hire you in any case unless they were absolutely desperate!" Tia commented—and Claire laughed, good-naturedly.

They talked on into the night, Tia saying several times that all she wanted was to sit back and relish her new found happiness without having her mind careening down about six other paths because of all these complications. Finally she said, "But how could I take this job anyway? Jimmy is going to need me to help out with Mavis."

"No!" Claire almost shouted. "It's actually providential if you have this to keep you occupied. It's too easy to fall into the role of caretaker and never get out again. Take it from me, but I don't have a choice. Take Jimmy at his word that he will make other arrangements. He loves you and I bet the last thing he wants is to risk you feeling like you are just useful to him. And, besides, you have Mario to think of."

"But I am sure he can't afford staff all the time even if he can get them. And what if they turn out to be unreliable like Amy? If he has to keep staying home with her or leaving work early, he could end up losing his job."

"You apply for the position and I will work hard on helping Jimmy to work through the PDD funding process. We'll get Intake out next week and when they see how disabled Mavis is, I'm sure they will expedite her application."

"So I guess that means Mavis will have to stay with Jimmy permanently. And with Mario and me, there will hardly be room. She will have to have the master bedroom with her own bathroom. That would be best, I think. And then we'll have to raise the bathtub, like Jessie's tub, so we can bathe her more easily. I guess the rest of us can shower downstairs. And…"

"Hold on," Claire said. "That's not how it's going to play out if I have anything to do with it. Mavis will be near enough so you can drop by and see her any time you like but she's not going to live with you."

"Oh? What other ideas do you have?"

"Just leave it to me. I'm not ready to talk about it yet—and I need to have a word with Jimmy and to be part of that meeting with PDD."

"Your role is to organize all our lives and my role is to push a mop!" Tia said with some heat.

"It's not like that. I have the connections. You don't. And you have the skills and the references to get that job. I don't. We have to pool our strengths if we're going to work our way out of this mess so you two can be happily married and get on with your lives."

Tia was somewhat mollified by this last comment but then retorted, "It does not look like we're going to be able to be happily married any time soon with all this to deal with."

"No. Unfortunately, I think you may be right on that point."

"Well, there is one thing," Tia said thoughtfully. Jimmy asked me if I would look into getting an annulment so we could have a church wedding. Since we're going to have to delay marriage anyway, I might as well. You wouldn't happen to know a sympathetic priest who could facilitate the process for me, by any chance?"

"Well, as it happens I think I might," Claire responded.

"Wow, you are a never-ending source of connections. Anyone would think *you* were the Italian!"

"Right now what I think is that we should give it up for tonight and get some sleep. We can't work it all out right now and I'm tired. Since you were already exhausted when you got home three hours ago you must be close to dead now. Do you think you can sleep?"

"It depends. Are you really sure you can pull off some of these grand schemes you mentioned or is it more or less just idle talk at this point?"

"Let's say I'm 80% sure. I have already done a lot of thinking and problem-solving in my own mind. I just need to get some of the pieces to fall into place and that is why I have to talk to Jimmy tomorrow—alone."

Tia looked at her suspiciously but said nothing. They took their cups to the sink and went to bed. It was after one in the morning.

Chapter 18—Claire Wheels and Deals

The next morning at eight, Claire quietly called Jimmy on her cell to ask if she could come over and talk to him. Tia was still sleeping but she knew he would be up because of the care provider arriving. She went home to change first and got to Jimmy's house about nine. He looked at her questioningly but directed her to the living room. First she said hello to Mavis, though, who was quietly eating her breakfast with the assistance of an attractive young African woman speaking to her in French. Mavis did not seem to mind and she also seemed to recognize Claire and to be happy to see her.

"I've completed my guardianship forms and included a copy of my criminal record check. I'll drop the forms off with Marion when I take Mavis up to see Bill tomorrow. I want to keep her here today to settle in," Jimmy said. "Later, when Tia comes, we'll take her for a walk so she can see the neighborhood."

"When will you be taking her back to Calgary?"

"I don't think I'm going to take her back," Jimmy blurted. "It was wrong for her to be there to begin with. She should be with family."

"What about Tia? Congratulations, by the way," Claire said drily. "I heard the news."

"Uh, thanks." Jimmy just nodded his head briefly but Claire saw the happy little smirk that lit up his face. "And I don't think Tia will mind," Jimmy continued. "We've already talked about it a little. And Mavis does not have to live with us. She just needs to be close—if I can set something up."

"Well, that's what I'm here to talk to you about," said Claire. "I have a few ideas I wanted to run by you to see what you think."

Jimmy raised his eyebrows questioningly and his body language indicated that he did not want any interference in his life, a point he'd made abundantly clear to Claire on previous occasions.

"Just hear me out, please, Jimmy. After all, I do have some experience in these matters. Let's just review the facts, okay?"

Jimmy nodded.

"You're the guardian for Mavis and the co-guardian for Bill. Marion has a heart condition and is not looking good. You could be left with sole oversight for Bill any time. If that happens, you're also going to want formal trusteeship so you can keep whatever financial resources he has available and use them to his best advantage. I assume you already have formal trusteeship for Mavis?"

Jimmy nodded but said nothing.

"If you want Mavis to live nearby but not with you," Claire continued, "then a logical roommate would be Bill. PDD is not going to provide 24/7 support for Mavis alone and even with Bill, they may still insist you take on a third person. That could be a problem as long as Bill has this murder charge hanging over him. People are going to think twice about placing a vulnerable son or daughter in the same house as him."

Jimmy did interject at this point. "Funny you should say that. I had a phone message from Roscoe's dad waiting when we got back last night. Roscoe was one of the guys who always sat at Bill's dining table at Forbes. You may recall meeting him the time you were there?"

"Oh, I remember that visit alright," Claire said wryly. She was recalling the embarrassing incident when she came close to being asked to leave and the role that Bill and his table partners had played in it. "But I don't recall who was who of the rest of them.

"Well, Roscoe's dad, Fuji, just retired and he and his wife want to move up to Edmonton to be closer to their older son who lives here with his wife."

"Roscoe's dad is called Fuji? Is Roscoe the Asian guy?"

"Yes. He's the one with Down syndrome. You didn't notice?"

"Well, how could you tell, the eyes and all—since he is Asian?"

Jimmy looked at Claire but did not say anything. *Funny*, he thought, *how even the most dedicated advocates for people with disabilities can have their blind spots and stereotypes.*

"Anyway," he said, they don't want to leave Roscoe alone at the Forbes Centre and Fuji was asking my advice about possible placements here in Edmonton. I know *they* would not be afraid to have Roscoe living with Bill. Bill and Roscoe have always gotten along really well."

"That's great!" Claire said excitedly. "Now, here's my plan! Have you noticed that Moira's house across the street is up for sale? From what Tia told me from her recollection of her brief time there cleaning and snooping before Moira caught her, it's more or less a duplicate of this house except there's a jet bath in the master bedroom and a bath/shower in the main bathroom. You could buy or rent that house, or if Mavis and Bill have any money of their own they could maybe buy it together. This Roscoe person could either buy in or pay rent and that would help cover the mortgage. Mavis could have the master bedroom and bath so she would have sufficient privacy and staff could use her bathroom since, apart from the tub, she won't have much use for it. "The guys could use the shower in the other bathroom since they can both walk." Then Mavis and Bill would be close so you could check on them easily and Roscoe's family could maybe do some of the work involved. And you need to get busy and make an offer now before somebody else snaps it up!"

Jimmy looked stunned. He knew Claire and knew she had a take charge kind of personality but he was not fully aware of the crafty turns her mind could take or the impulsivity of her nature. If Claire's husband, Dan, had been there he would have been smirking at this point. This was so typically Claire!

After taking a moment to absorb all this, Jimmy replied slowly and thoughtfully, "It could be a solution. I'd love to have her that close but I'd want some time for Tia and me too, so her not living with us but living that near to us would be ideal. But I wonder if Moira's daughter will even sell it to us under the circumstances?"

"I thought of that," Claire said. "That's why I think it would be good to put it in Bill's and Mavis's names, assuming they have the resources. *They* are not responsible for the fact that her mother is now in jail for murdering your wife! That also avoids any tax implications for you down the road. And, worst case scenario, you can pay her more than the asking price. I only met her once but, if I have read her correctly, *that* should get to her!"

"There is that small matter of Bill facing a murder charge. If the neighbors get wind of it they might object and raise a big stink about having a group home on the street."

"That's why we have to work on clearing his name––because we certainly cannot expect McCoy to do it. In his lazy, arrogant way, he figures he already has his man—or, as he puts it, his boy!"

Jimmy nodded in agreement but then added "How do you plan to do that?" From what I heard there aren't too many loose ends to follow up."

Claire replied triumphantly, "I just came up with a plan for that this weekend. The Clive Center is applying for housekeeping assistance on the third floor, the same floor where Bill was. I figure Tia…"

"*Ooh*, no!" Jimmy stood up in agitation, interrupting her. "You are *not* going to rope Tia into this, get her snooping around with a murderer on the loose. *Absolutely not!?!*"

"I already emailed in my application this morning," Tia said quietly. She had come in unnoticed and heard the last exchange.

"I don't want you to do it!" Jimmy said stubbornly. It's not safe!"

"Well, I *am* going to do it," Tia asserted with equal stubbornness. I promised Claire last night that I would and in any case we have to do something to help Bill and Marion!"

"I insist…" Jimmy started to say.

Tia held up her hand, palm out, and her eyes flashed angrily. "First of all, you can't. You have no authority over me or direct say in my life as of yet. Secondly," she added in a meeker tone, "can we please wait at least until I get my ring before we have our first fight?" She pushed tears out of her eyes but put her chin up and held her ground.

"Oh!" Claire said cheerily, in a frantic effort to defuse the situation. "When are you going ring shopping?"

"I would like to be doing that right now—and to be having this argument in private," Jimmy said, with his arms now firmly around Tia. But I don't want to leave Mavis alone with the new care provider."

"Well, that is one problem I can solve," Claire chuckled. "Andrea is with Jessie today. She works every second Sunday and is much more attuned to Jessie than Amy has ever been. Therefore, I'm free as a bird until four this afternoon. You two need some time together. Just get out of here. Have lunch. Go ring shopping. Talk. I can manage everything here better than even you could, Jimmy!"

"I have no doubt of that," Jimmy said, grinning. "But really? Are you sure?"

"Positive. Consider it an early shower gift. It is a crime for the two of you to be standing here caught up in all these worries when you are just newly engaged. Just tell me what food you have in mind for Mavis' lunch. I can prepare it. And if you don't have anything I will run home and get one of Jessie's meals."

"No need. I'm prepared," Jimmy said. "And thanks, Claire. I really appreciate this. I'll talk to Tia about the matters we discussed this morning and we will consider this cleaning job business but I need to find out more about it—and there better not be any night hours!" he ended ominously.

Chapter 19—the Ring and the Rumble

Jimmy's home was in the Lendrum area of Edmonton so it was a short drive to the Southgate Shopping Center. There were three different jewelry shops there and Tia and Jimmy carefully examined all the rings. "They seem to be very expensive," Tia said nervously. Maybe we should check around, look online—wait awhile."

"No!" Jimmy declared. "Assuming you find one you like here, I want this settled today. I won't be able to get away again easily. Besides," he added with a sly smile, "I want to put my mark on you. I want others to know you are taken!"

Tia grinned happily. They went back through the three shops again but she kept returning to one of them and looking at a particular ring. It had a plain but elegantly shaped white gold band with a half carat raised solitaire diamond mounted on it.

"You like that ring, don't you?" Jimmy said softly.

"I do—although I see there are less expensive ones I could probably like just as well."

"Yes, let's look some more,"—and he pointed silently to the shop attendant to retrieve the ring next to it. It was identical except that instead of a half carat diamond it had a full carat one.

Tia looked at the ring and then at the price, almost twice that of the first one, and said, "No, if you really think this one with the smaller diamond does not cost too much, I would prefer it. The other one is just too big and showy for me. I would not be comfortable wearing it."

"The deal was soon concluded and the ring left behind, regretfully, for sizing. The clerk assured him it would be ready in two days and Jimmy took a picture of it on Tia's finger with his cell phone so she could show Claire. He grinned secretly to himself when they finally walked away. He was learning how to get around Tia. Faced with the choice between the two rings, she was so busy defending the smaller one that she forgot about the cheaper ones she had vowed to settle for!

Over lunch at the food fair (Tia insisted on this choice in reaction to the cost of the ring), Jimmy shared with her Claire's ideas on living arrangements for Mavis and Bill and Roscoe.

"That sounds really good to me!" Tia said. "I want to be able to check on Mavis at least a couple of times a day and it would be nice not to have to jump in the car to do it. But then she added, "We're assuming that we'll find an agency willing to take Bill on. That may not be so easy."

"I have a feeling Claire probably has that covered, too. She seems to have thought of everything else!" Jimmy chuckled. After a pause he added, "Let's talk about this job, Tia. I really am not comfortable with you doing it. Remember what happened last time you went snooping around a murderer? You almost got killed! I can't lose you now. Please see it from my point of view," Jimmy pleaded.

"Just let me go to the interview and find out what's involved. I can promise you one thing. I'm not going to work nights. I couldn't anyway, because of Mario."

"Okay— but if anything happens to you, I will kill the son of a bitch," Jimmy said fiercely. "And then I will probably go to jail for the rest of my life so think what would happen to Mavis and Bill then!"

Tia smiled at his fervor. "I don't want to lose you either—and I also have to think of Mario. So, of course, I'll be careful. I know, for example, that nobody there puts their last name on their name tags and no personal information is available on the unit. That's all locked up in the Human Resources office. And I'll make sure I'm not followed when I leave!" she added, with a naughty grin.

"Not funny," Jimmy growled, but they moved onto other subjects—and they had many subjects to cover.

Chapter 20—Life Changes

On the drive to school Monday morning, Mario asked his grand-father, "When did you start painting, Nonno?"

"I only started after I retired. Before that I was too busy trying to earn a living!"

"Why did you decide to paint?"

"I wanted to paint Alberta skies. They are so clear and so big and always different. You can get lost in them."

Mario thought about this and told his grandfather about the Picasso exhibit he'd seen with Aunty Claire. "Can we visit the new Art Gallery of Alberta together some time, Nonno?" Alberto agreed that that would be a good idea.

Mario and his grandparents had talked about a lot of things that weekend but Mario had been careful not to talk about his plan to bring his mother and Jimmy together, just in case it didn't work. But when he arrived home from school that evening, his mother informed him that Jimmy was coming over for dinner. Claire had agreed to visit with Mavis and the assistant that evening, so Tia and Jimmy could tell Mario about their engagement.

"Okay," he said, as nonchalantly as he could, and then ran off to his room so she would not see the grin on his face.

The evening went well and Mario took the news with surprising equanimity. After dinner, Tia left the two of them alone so she could wash the dishes and clean up the kitchen. Mario was enjoying talking to Jimmy and he told him about his grandfather's painting.

"I used to paint," Jimmy told him. "Maybe someday I will get the chance to talk to your Nonno about painting. I don't know anybody else who paints, so that would be really interesting."

"Do you think you would like to start painting again, sir?"

"*Sir?*"

"Well, what would you like me to call you, Mr. Elves?

"I don't know. What would *you* like to call me?

"Well, you're going to be like my dad, now, aren't you?" The normally self-possessed Mario blushed when he said this and reverted to the vernacular of his peer group in order to defuse it somewhat.

"I really want to be your dad but that honor has gone to somebody else, hasn't it?"

"But he has never been like a real dad to me!"

"Still, he gave you something."

"What?"

"Your mother says you got your brain from him."

"But brains aren't everything," said Mario, the well-rehearsed line that had been drilled into him by his mother for as long as he could remember.

"Still, it's a very special gift but, of course, with that comes an extra weight of responsibility to do your best to make a difference in the world. What would you like to be when you grow up?"

"I don't know yet, but I think we're getting away from the original subject, aren't we?"

"Yes, what would you like to call me then?"

"Mario put his head down to hide another blush and mumbled, "could I just call you Jim-Dad?"

"Sounds very Southern but also kind of original, the kind of thing a guy like you would come up with. I would be okay with that. I would be proud to be seen as even partly your father."

"Or I could just call you JD, like initials you know. And then *they* wouldn't know what I was saying but you and I would."

"Yes, but the trouble with that is I would *want* everyone to know I was your dad or partly your dad, anyway, and then they wouldn't know."

"Well," Mario hung his head shyly, "maybe after I call you Jim-Dad for a while it will get kind of awkward and we will both feel it's easier if I just call you Dad. I guess it's a process!"

"Yeah—I think you're right. Now here is something else for you to consider. Would you be willing to take my last name so the world would know that you belong to me now and we are a family? I would like to adopt you."

"Yes! Then we can all be Elves and then if I have a little sister she will have the same last name as me and people will know she's my sister!" Mario said all this in a tone that expressed great relief and Jimmy realized sadly that he'd been quietly worrying about this issue."

Chapter 21—the Hard Working Life

Tia had emailed in her application on Monday morning and the Human Resources office had called her later that day to set up an interview for Tuesday morning. The interview went smoothly. Tia's references had already been checked and she saw as soon as she walked in that they were very happy to have her application. Before she left, she was told that the job was hers if she wanted it. She thought for a moment about whether or not she would check with Jimmy before accepting it but instead asked about the hours. It was a part-time position from 10-3, ideal in terms of Mario's schedule. The days were generally Mondays, Wednesdays and Fridays but during weeks when a Statutory Holiday fell on one of those days, the schedule was shifted so they could get around paying a 2.5 rate. Keeping the position at 15 hours a week also meant that they did not have to pay benefits. Tia saw all this and felt sorry for the others who worked there because they had no better options. But for her purposes it was ideal. She was hopefully not going to be staying that long in any case. After quickly assessing the situation, Tia agreed to the position and signed the necessary papers. They asked her to report the very next day for training. She just hoped that Jimmy would not be too upset with her.

Tia was there at nine the next morning as agreed and she was assigned to a partner to orient her to the routine. Elsie Petrosky was clearly not impressed. She looked up and down at Tia and observed her small, unreddened hands, her shapely, unbroken nails, even the precise crease down the front of her well-fitting jeans. "Kanadisch," she sneered to herself. Tia, on the other hand, was wondering what she'd gotten herself into as she observed the quintessential washerwoman type in front of her.

"Ve start here," Elsie informed Tia, in a harsh voice. "You vash all, yeah?" She pointed up and down the hall, waving her hand to indicate every room and stomped the mop on the floor."

"Where do I get clean water and soap when I need to change it?" Tia asked. The woman looked at her uncomprehendingly. "More water," Tia repeated, and she pantomimed dumping the water out and filling the pail again.

"No-o," the woman said and pointed at the pail. "Das vater. Enough."

Tia shook her head and started off. Predictably, once she had mopped two rooms on each side and the piece of the hall that joined them, the water was a decided shade of brown. She looked dispiritedly at the pail and scanned the hall for her mentor but she was not to be seen. *What now?* she asked herself. Then a piece of luck came her way. The head of housekeeping, who had earlier introduced herself to Tia as Beulah Twain, came walking briskly down the hall. Tia waylaid her and explained the problem, pointing at the dirty pail of water for emphasis. The woman pointed out where she could get the necessary supplies but warned her that there were three other units to mop down after this so she could not be too particular or she would run out of time. Tia's only response to that was that she also had a second concern. She needed some tools so she could deal with the build-up of sludge that the mop had swirled into the corners; a thin plastering spatula might work but she would also need some of those new Mr. Clean eraser blocks so she could scrub away the remaining residue and also use them to get the line of dirt out that had become ingrained in the top of the tall, wooden baseboards. In addition, she could use some old towels to wrap around the mop so that with a pail of clean water and soap she could efficiently swab down the baseboards without leaving marks on the plaster walls above. The woman reminded her again about the time line and Tia responded, "Okay, I may do that another day when I get an earlier start. They won't have to be done every time. Once every couple of weeks should do and once I get the corners clean they should stay that way. I'll just carry along a piece of toweling and dry the corners with my foot on it as I go."

"We'll see how much you get done today," the woman said doubtfully and left.

By three o'clock, Tia had cleaned all the floors on level three, as requested of her, and they shone in a way they obviously had not for a long time. She was reasonably satisfied but vowed she would get to work on the corners her very next shift and the baseboards after that. Tia ran into Beulah Twain again just as she was finishing off the floors in the last unit. "All done!" Tia said cheerfully. The woman gazed up and down the hall and smiled. Within a week, Tia was in charge of training staff on her floor and assigning the cleaning tasks according to her own system of priorities that she had developed. Elsie Petrosky had left in a huff!

Tia accepted that perfection was not possible given the limited resources available but had also quickly recognized that the cleaning could be a lot more efficient and thorough than it had been without necessarily overworking anyone. Beulah Twain loved her; her coworkers not so much.

Chapter 22—Where Do We Go From Here?

One night Tia was visiting with Claire who naturally asked her what she had learned. "Well, I had to wrap my head around the job and establish my legitimacy first, didn't I?" Tia responded.

"Are the other staff friendly with you? Do you think they will talk to you?"

"They do seem a bit cool, actually," Tia admitted. "I think the problem is that some of them have been cleaning in the same haphazard way for a long time and then I came along and changed things."

"Don't you think maybe that you are losing sight of the purpose of this whole exercise, Tia? You weren't supposed to transform the hygiene standards of the Clive Centre. You were supposed to try to find out who killed that nurse."

"I can't help it," Tia said. "I have to do things my own way. I'll begin working seriously on the other part this coming week. But I have made one friend there, and she's responsible for cleaning in the unit where Bill was staying. She's really into cleaning properly, too, so she likes the changes I've made. I can't say the same for some of the others who seem to resent me and try to avoid me."

"Well, unless you have ambitions of making a career out of housekeeping at the Clive Centre, I suggest that you stop cleaning so much and start digging."

"Will do, boss!" Tia said cheerfully. "By the way, I did see one interesting thing. I was coming out of the elevator today and I saw a man and a woman arguing at the end of the hall. When I got closer to them, I saw that it was Frankie Jessick. Denise pointed him out to me once in the cafeteria. And I think the woman was Jennie Marlowe but I'm not certain. She had stomped off before I got close enough to see for sure."

"*That's* the sort of thing you need to be focusing on– –not dust bunnies! Keep it up!" Claire replied.

Chapter 23—Tia Gets to Work

Tia and Denise, her new friend, were enjoying a coffee break together at work. Denise was an attractive black woman with a beautiful musical lilt to her voice. Tia said, "I gather from your accent that you are from the West Indies. Which island?"

"Barbados."

"Oh," Tia replied. "I heard that that woman who was killed was also from Barbados. Are there others here on staff from there? I know it's a pretty small country so it's quite a coincidence to even have the two of you here."

"Well, I'm here because my uncle came over five years ago and he's one of the security guards. He told me they were always looking for housekeeping staff here so I applied. I told them if they would bring me over on the Foreign Workers Program I would commit to staying for at least two years, assuming my work visa did not expire. And that would be their problem to make sure that did not happen. There's a certain amount of bookwork involved."

"Anybody else here on that program?" Tia asked casually.

Denise looked at her sharply and replied reluctantly. "Yeah, there's Frankie Jessick. He works afternoons and nights in 3-B." Tia involuntarily raised her eyebrows, registering that this was the same unit where Annette Richards had been killed. Denise caught the response and added defensively, "But his family lives on the other side of the island from her. I asked him about it and he said that he and Annette did not know each other before he came. He's only been here about five months but she was here two or three years. They didn't socialize. She probably thought she was out of his league being a nurse and all while he's just an orderly. Besides, she was married to some white guy. I heard some of the others talking about it and they said that's how she got over here so easily and got the job she did. Lots of times nurses come over to work in places like this but they get hired on as LPN's even though they are fully qualified. Apparently, her husband has some kind of pull here so that didn't happen to her. She was even the charge nurse at times and, according to the gossip, liked to lord it over people."

"Interesting," Tia said. "Thanks for sharing. It makes my job a little easier if I understand the politics. My own family came over from Italy and I know all about what it's like to be treated as a second class citizen. I hate that kind of snobbery. I like to treat everybody the same."

"We've all noticed that," Denise said. "A lot of the others resent you for making the changes you have and causing more work for them but they all have to acknowledge that you're not just bossing others around. You're working just as hard yourself."

"I like hard work and I like people who are hard working. I can see that you are like that, too, Denise. I have a tough time with slackers. I want to yell at them to shape up or ship out or just plain fire them since a leopard does not usually change its spots. But I can't really do that in the position I'm in here. It's kind of frustrating."

"Well, if you think you find things frustrating among the housekeeping staff, you should have been here when Annette Richards was alive. Not nice to speak ill of the dead, but the fact is she was bone lazy and sneaky and conniving enough to get away with it."

"I bet that got to the people who had to work with her," Tia said casually. "She mustn't have been too popular."

"Oh, nobody liked her much that I know of, although occasionally she'd butter up to somebody and throw some perks their way so she'd have an ally if she needed one. Anyway, nobody could say much or report her because she was the boss and quite capable of making their lives miserable. One of the other nurses *did* report her for sleeping at night when she was on duty and leaving the orderly alone to monitor the situation but she only had hearsay evidence since she did not work the same shift. When Ivy Watson, the unit manager, came to question people about this, nobody would back Kari up and Annette convinced Ivy that Kari was just jealous and trying to cause grief for her. And the next day, Annette got even. It must have been when she came in for the afternoon shift. Kari's car was still there because the shifts overlap—you know to allow for information exchange. When Kari came out to go home, she found her rear wheel well bashed right in and the next day somebody told her that they'd seen some red paint on Annette's bumper. By the time Kari got a chance to check out Annette's bumper, there was no paint on it but she did see a dull patch where it had been sanded down. So nobody could ever prove anything but everybody knew. That happened a couple of months ago and I don't think anybody tried to cross Annette after that."

Tia looked at her watch and said, "Well, this has all been very interesting, Denise, but I guess it's time we both got back to work. Thanks for sharing, though. I'm not much in the loop around here yet, since everybody else seems a bit standoffish. If you get the chance, put in a good word for me, eh? I'm not that bad." Denise agreed heartily and said that she would.

Chapter 24—Tia and Claire Plan Their Strategy

That evening Claire came over to see Tia after both Jessie and Mario were in bed for the night. As usual, they sat at Tia's kitchen table drinking coffee, in this case, de-caf, and enjoying slices of Tia's latest cake. She informed Claire that she'd bought a copy of Jean Paré's[iii] cake cookbook and was working her way through it systematically. This time it was beet cake. Claire grinned. This approach to baking was certainly odd but it was so Tia!

Together they discussed what Denise had said, what they could do to follow up on the information and whether or not they should inform Inspector McCoy. "I don't trust him," Tia said, "and we better be careful he does not find us snooping around or even learn that I'm working at Clive."

"Maybe we could mention it to Sergeant Crombie. I could see that he wasn't happy about how quickly McCoy concluded that Bill was the murderer. He might at least give us some ideas on how to proceed and I'm pretty sure he would not rat us out."

"Maybe," Tia said. "Do you think he'd be able to check up on the background of this Frankie Jessick character? Maybe even Annette's husband? Darn! I forgot to ask her his name!"

They talked some more, weighing the pros and cons of telling Sergeant Crombie since they'd learned the hard way last time about the importance of keeping under the radar. But they were both tired from a long day so decided they'd better call it a night and sleep on it before making any decision.

While Tia had been busy establishing a place for herself at her new job, Claire had also been busy. She had been in contact with CARP and lined up a volunteer lawyer who was supposedly expediting the guardianship papers and had also gotten Marion and Jimmy to fill out the papers necessary to share formal trusteeship for Bill. Marion had resisted at first, feeling if anyone else should have control over Bill's money matters it should be Hilda so they could keep it in the family. Hilda was currently the co-trustee but had agreed only grudgingly and when she found out that Jimmy was willing to take it on she was quick to back out, reciting her stock line: "I've got my own things to do!"

Mavis had now been living with Jimmy for more than two weeks and Claire could see it was wearing on him. He was rapidly using up holiday time so he could leave work an hour early each day. Also, he'd told Tia that to pay the staff at the rate of $27.00 per hour, roughly twice the rate of private hiring because of the agency fee involved, he'd used up all the money Megan had left and was now working through the money in Mavis's AISH account.

Meanwhile, Marion was continuing to spend long hours at the hospital every day and living under the ongoing stress and fear that Bill would have a big blow-up and make the case against him even worse. Jimmy had managed to bring Mavis up a few times and, of course, Bill was delighted to see her but he always got so upset when it was time for her to leave that they all feared a major meltdown. Jimmy was showing the strain of the whole affair almost as much as Marion.

Claire reviewed these matters in her mind and then went over a half dozen related issues that were also present. She felt like she was swimming against a very strong current and was in serious danger of going under before she reached shore. She resolved that the best way to move forward was to deal with one issue at a time and she decided to focus on what she considered to be a particularly pressing one—Mavis' toileting situation. Tia had told her that there was now a constant faint smell of dirty diaper residue in the house and Jimmy was finding it very annoying and embarrassing to the point where he did not even want Tia to come over any more. And Jimmy could not leave the house in the evening because most of the time he did not have care providers after four, given the cost involved—and those he did have were substitute workers he did not want to leave alone with Mavis. "I've neglected her for too long," he said to Tia. "No more!"

"This is ridiculous," Claire said angrily. "I'm going to deal with the toileting issue this week and find a solution."

Chapter 25—Once You Learn to Ride a Bicycle

The next day, Claire hauled over to Jimmy's house a new commode modified for Jessie by seating specialists but never really workable because it was just a little too big for her. Claire was gratified to see that Mavis could sit on it comfortably and securely. A ceiling lift was already in place since, at Claire's suggestion, Jimmy had contacted AADL, the Alberta Aids to Daily Living Program, for assistance as soon as he had decided that Mavis would remain in Edmonton. The track for the lift made it easy to transfer Mavis from her bed to her wheelchair and now to the new commode.

The rest of the day, Claire was preoccupied with attending to the decorating needs of her few remaining clients, but the next morning Claire arrived at Jimmy's house at 7:30. Dan had agreed to get Jessie off to school, not without a certain amount of grumbling. But Claire had stood her ground, stating over and over that the toileting issue for Mavis was too important to put off and that only she could make it happen. Jimmy was getting ready for work when Claire arrived and Mavis was still asleep but Claire gently woke her up, undressed her and slipped the toileting sling under her legs. Then she swung Mavis across from the bed to the commode, straightened her out on the seat and strapped her in securely. She tucked a towel under the lap strap for privacy. "Pee, Mavis," Claire instructed. "I know you can. Go pee!" and Claire stroked Mavis' hand gently. She heard the doorbell ring but, as prearranged with Jimmy, he kept the care provider in the kitchen and away from Mavis. Claire did not want to introduce any distractions at this delicate stage.

Mavis sat on the commode for several minutes with nothing happening and Claire was about ready to give up when there was a tinkling sound on the bottom of the commode pot. Mavis got a shocked look on her face and it stopped. Claire encouraged her and in another minute it happened again and the third time Mavis let go entirely, emptying her bladder. Claire was beside herself with joy! She hugged Mavis and praised her and then cleaned her and moved her to the bed and dressed her and hugged her and praised her some more. The other two came into the room and did the same. Mavis grinned happily.

Every two hours throughout the day, Claire continued this routine with Mavis, sometimes succeeding, and sometimes failing. Then, just shortly before the assistant was scheduled to leave at four, Mavis became very agitated. Claire and the assistant checked her for fever and felt her stomach to see if she had cramps. Suddenly Claire smacked her head with her hand. "Mavis, do you need to go to the bathroom?" Mavis stopped fussing momentarily, and moved her finger tentatively towards her mouth. "Yes, I think that's what you need!" Claire quickly undressed Mavis and placed her on the commode. After buckling her in securely, Claire told Mavis that she would leave her alone for some privacy. But she had not reached the door before she realized something was happening.

Just then the front door opened and Jimmy walked in. "Well, I gather there's still a ways to go with your project, Claire," he said, wrinkling his nose.

"Not true," Claire responded. "We just did not think to wheel the commode into the bathroom but we will next time. Mavis let us know just like you said! I *knew* she could do it!" Claire crowed. "You can never forget something as fundamental as that. It's like learning to ride a bicycle. You never forget once you know how!"

Jimmy was thrilled, so thrilled that in his mind he forgave Claire for all her past interference. Claire left then, very tired after the intensive efforts of the day. She left instructions with Jimmy to toilet Mavis every two hours or whenever he saw her put her finger in her mouth. Within a week, Mavis was responding as if she had not been away from her toileting regimen for the past 20 years!

Chapter 26— Aunt Gus Weighs In

The next morning, Claire decided it was time to check in with her Aunt Augusta. She'd been too busy to call her for quite a while now and was feeling increasingly guilty about it. Gus, as Augusta insisted on being called, was Claire's deceased mother's younger sister. She was widowed and living in Calgary on her own with just her two cats for company. She and Marion had been friends, but now Marion had moved away, too.

"Hello, whose calling?"

"Aunt Gus, this is Claire. How are you?"

"Busy!" It did not occur to Gus to ask about Claire. That was not her way.

"What are you up to?"

"Moving."

"Moving? When? Where?"

"Edmonton. I'll be living with Amanda for the time being. I'm putting my furniture in storage there—just in case we don't get along and I need to get my own place." Amanda Roche was the elderly lady who lived next door to Jimmy. She and Aunt Gus, working together, had played a significant role in cracking the case against him.

"Well, you're always welcome to live with us. You know that," Claire said feebly.

"I doubt that that surly husband of yours would agree with you."

"You're not being fair to Dan. I know he was pretty annoyed with you but he had his reasons, didn't he? But he would never object to you living with me. After all, you're the only family I have left!"

"Well, whether Dan thinks he could put up with me or not, I'm not interested. I'm going to live with Amanda. That will be better for everybody."

Claire decided she was getting into a no-win situation and it was time to change the subject. "But when are you planning to come to Edmonton then?"

The moving company is loading up the van tomorrow morning and I'll be taking a 5 pm Westjet flight. I'll be getting in about 5:45."

Claire was silent for a minute and then said, "When were you planning to tell me this, Aunt Gus?"

"I've been busy," she said, and then, dimly realizing that this might come across as offensive, added lamely, "I thought I would surprise you!" After a few seconds to allow her mental wheels to turn over, she went on. "Of course, since you had to phone today and ruin the surprise, you might as well pick me up at the airport. It is a pretty stiff taxi fare otherwise, you know, and I *am* on pension!"

Claire thought a minute. "I guess I could do that. "And Aunt Gus?"

"What"

"I'm really glad you're going to be living in Edmonton so I can see you more often."

"Yes, well my arthritis is getting worse and with Marion gone, I figured I better be around somebody who knows me in case I need help," she said, matter of factly. Only after she hung up the phone did it occur to her that she might have returned Claire's sentiment—but she did not want to admit that she was lonely.

It was four o'clock. *Tia should be home*, Claire thought. When Claire got her on the phone she let loose. Aunt Gus could be outrageous but this was surely the limit. Did she not care at all about Claire and Jessie?

Forget that garbage about surprise. That was not her style. Her style was to contact Claire only when she needed something. Otherwise, why waste a dollar on an unnecessary phone call?

After about five minutes of venting, Tia finally interjected. "Come on, Claire. Consider the source. She has about as much social skill as your average pigeon! If she's going to live here, you'll have to develop a thicker skin. And," Tia added, "just be glad she did not take you up on your lame offer to have her live with you! She knows Dan would not want her there and she's probably just trying to protect herself from feeling rejected by acting so cool and independent."

"Well, if you put it that way," Claire sniffed, and marveled once more at how Tia could always put things in perspective and make her feel better.

Chapter 27—Aunt Gus Gets in on the Act

On the way home from the airport, Claire updated Gus on the murder and what had happened to Bill. Predictably, she was shocked and demanded to know why she'd not been told. Claire thought this was pretty rich considering what Gus had just pulled off, but answered sedately. "If you'd called me to inquire about his well-being or to ask how Marion was doing, I certainly would have told you. But as you say, you've been too busy to bother with any of us!" Claire could not resist getting this little dig in because she was still feeling somewhat hurt. She noted with satisfaction that Aunt Gus had the grace to blush.

Gus was quiet for a moment and then, in a belated effort to express some degree of social concern, asked how Jimmy was doing.

"He's happy but getting very tired. Mavis is living with him now, you know." Claire risked taking her eyes off the road for a few seconds to sneak a furtive peak at Aunt Gus to see how she was taking it. She looked set back on her heels which Claire found very satisfying. *Payback!* she said to herself.

But Gus took the opportunity to act quite umbraged. "Well, it certainly wasn't very considerate of you not to tell me. I was planning to go up there and see Mavis before I left so I could tell Jimmy how she was, but then I got too busy. Good thing or I would have wasted two taxi fares for nothing!"

Claire said nothing but smiled to herself. She very much doubted that Aunt Gus would have expended even one taxi fare on such a project or that the idea would have even occurred to her. However, Claire thought she'd better start getting on the same page if she wanted some assistance, which she did.

"Oh, I don't know if I already mentioned it but Tia and Jimmy are engaged!"

"No, you certainly did not! Tell me all about it." Gus looked to be almost purring at the thought of sharing a juicy bit of gossip and participating second hand in Tia's romance.

"They went to Calgary together a couple of weeks ago to pick Mavis up and it happened on the way. Actually, her son asked me not to go so his mother would have to. I think he was pretty sure that the two of them could not hold out alone together in a car for three or four hours and he was right! You'll have to meet this kid, Aunt Gus. He will change your mind about not liking children!"

"Amanda already told me about him. He sounds like a smart kid and a real character. That was a pretty clever strategy!" Gus laughed. "Go on, tell me more. What kind of a ring did he get her?"

"By the way," Claire asked, abruptly changing the subject. "Did you get rid of that nice German hutch and buffet unit you had?"

It took a few seconds for Gus to get back on that track. "No, I remembered how much you liked that set so I figured I better keep it in case you wanted it someday when I am gone." Actually, Gus had only remembered how much Claire admired the hutch and buffet combination at the moment when Claire asked the question and that factor had not entered remotely into her calculations. She had kept the unit because there was not the time to find a buyer who would pay her what she knew it was worth. But by this time, she was dimly aware that Claire was feeling hurt. Self-centered as she was, Gus was not entirely without feeling. If the promise of a piece of furniture could take away the hurt she had apparently caused, then Gus had no regrets—especially since she'd had the foresight to offer it only after she was dead.

Claire smiled and said, "Thanks for thinking of me, Aunt Gus."

Gus had an uncomfortable twinge inside, realizing herself the extent of her own thoughtlessness. She really did care about Claire but somehow she was always so wrapped up in her own concerns that Claire and Jessie rarely entered her awareness.

Chapter 28—Aunt Gus Stakes her Claim

Gus arrived at Amanda Roche's door with her purse in one hand and a cat carrier in the other. Claire staggered along behind her with Gus's oversized suitcase.

"Did you really need to bring all this stuff with you right now, Aunt Gus, when the moving van is arriving tomorrow?" Claire asked, as she struggled to hump the huge suitcase up the steps.

"No, but it was just as easy to bring it since the airline carried it for free. It cuts down on the moving costs a bit. They go by weight you know. This way I saved paying for 30 kilos!"

Claire said nothing but thought to herself, *Easy for you; not so much for me. Typical!*

"Oh, there you are!" Amanda greeted Gus when she opened the door. Looking over her shoulder, she saw Claire and greeted her as well. "I haven't seen you for a long time, Claire. How are you doing?"

"Apart from having a sore arm right now, I'm fine," Claire said wryly. "How's life with you, Amanda?"

"Good. I've been busy though. I had to clean out an extra bedroom for your aunt and the closet was jam packed with all my spare clothes. It gave me a good opportunity to get rid of stuff I didn't need." By this time they were in the allotted room and Claire parked the suitcase with a sigh of relief.

Gus opened the closet door and peeked inside. "Oh, I'll never get all my clothes in there," she complained. "You really should have switched rooms with me,

Amanda. Your wardrobe needs are pretty modest and you don't need that double closet in there." Claire winced visibly at this outrageous remark but Gus actually thought she'd put it quite diplomatically. She hadn't mentioned that she was considerably more sophisticated in her tastes than Amanda, for example.

"I may not need it," Amanda responded tartly, "but this is my house and that has been my bedroom for the past 30 years. I'm not going to change rooms now!"

"Oh, well," Gus muttered. "I guess I can put my armoire in the other bedroom and keep the clothes I don't wear every day in there." By this time, the cats were meowing fiercely and Gus made a move to let them out.

"I have their own litter box ready for them on the back stairs landing," Amanda said.

"Oh, I just let them go outside to do their business," Gus responded. "That way I don't have to clean a litter box."

"Not *here*, they won't! I don't want them digging in my flower beds and making a mess in the yard."

Claire could see that things were coming to a head, so she quickly interjected. "You know what, Aunt Gus? I think I better take the cats home with me right now to give you a chance to settle in," and she stood up to go.

"I'll carry the litter box to the car for you," Amanda said, and Claire detected a note of gratitude in her voice.

Gus started to protest but Claire stopped her with a warning note in her voice. "It's better this way, Aunt Gus. I'll see you tomorrow." She leaned over her chair and kissed her on the cheek and then left quickly with the cats in tow.

Chapter 29—Claire Gets Some New Recruits

The next morning at breakfast, Dan made it clear to Claire that he was not pleased with the presence of the cats. Claire informed him it was either them or Aunt Gus because otherwise the arrangement with Amanda was almost guaranteed to break down. And then she would have no other choice but to come to them. Claire added, "They just need time to adjust to each other without this additional irritant. I don't think the cats will be much trouble and Jessie might enjoy them." Meanwhile, the cats were managing to fit themselves into their temporary home very quickly and seemed quite content, even perhaps grateful, for the convenience of a litter box.

The next morning, since Jessie was at school for the day and Claire was at a low point in terms of clientele, she decided she better see how Amanda and Aunt Gus were getting on and to do any necessary trouble shooting there. Claire found the two ladies sitting companionably at the kitchen table with one of Amanda's cats on each of their laps. The atmosphere seemed decidedly more friendly and relaxed than it had the night before.

"How's everything?" Claire asked after sitting down with her own cup of coffee.

"We were just discussing furniture arrangements and how we can fit in a couple of Gus's nice pieces," Amanda said cheerfully.

"Amanda has a very nice basement which is high and dry and warm and airy but she does not have much use for it. And the plumbing for a two piece bath is already in place. I was talking about possibly doing renovations down there so I could have my own sitting room and in case our cats don't get along mine could stay down there. There are a couple of deep window ledges they could perch on and look out and I think they could enjoy that."

"Sounds good!" Claire said. "Well, I'm sure you'll work it out. Meanwhile, don't worry about your cats, Aunt Gus. They seem to be adapting quite nicely. And the brown faced one jumped up on Jessie's lap this morning and just sat there purring for a few minutes. It made Jessie laugh!"

"Oh, that's nice!" Gus and Amanda said in unison. Gus added, "I'm always happy to do something that helps Jessie," completely forgetting, in her usual egocentric way, that the arrangement had been made by Claire for the express purpose of helping *her*.

Amanda jumped in at this point and asked Claire to tell her all that was happening with the murder case. "Tell me who else but this Bill guy could have done it." Claire explained about the unit arrangements and about the two other staff members, Frankie and Jennie, who had been working that night.

"Are they married?" Gus asked.

"No, I don't think so," Claire responded. "Frankie is just here as a foreign worker and he'll be going back home to Barbados when his visa expires. Sergeant Crombie told me that Jennie still lives with her parents and she's 27. Apparently, it took her a long time to get through her practical nursing program."

"That's kind of old to be living at home, isn't it?" Amanda replied.

"Not in this day and age. Lots of young people stay at home with their parents until they can pay off their education loans."

"What can we do to help?" Gus broke in, eagerly. "You know we were able to help you quite a lot last time!"

This was the opportunity that Claire had been waiting for. "I know you always like to help where you can, Aunt Gus, but you know who really needs help right now? Jimmy. He doesn't want to leave Mavis alone with the care provider in case something happens so he's missing a lot of work running home all the time and using up all his holiday time. If he knew he could have the assistant call on you or Amanda when there was trouble and if you could just pop over there and visit once or twice a day it would really take a lot of pressure off him."

"*I* wouldn't mind helping out that way," Amanda said. Claire smiled to herself because she knew this would put pressure on Aunt Gus who had yet to respond. Undoubtedly, she was busy calculating what was in it for her but also would not like to look ungenerous in contrast to Amanda's quick and cheerful offer.

"When I get my cats here I could always bring them over. Mavis would probably enjoy them. Also, how about walks? The weather is pretty nice now. I could certainly do that. As you recall, I have had some practice taking Jessie out," Gus responded.

Claire said nothing but raised her eyebrows. She could think of a few past incidents which might suggest that this would not be a good idea but it seemed wiser not to mention them if she wanted to get some assistance for Jimmy. Instead, she said, "Well, the problem with walks right now is getting Mavis up and down the front steps in her wheelchair. I'm working on borrowing a folding steel ramp temporarily but until that happens, I'm afraid Mavis is kind of stuck in the house. It must get boring for her and for the assistant so

I'm sure they would appreciate your company." Claire favored them both with a grateful gaze. "Would you like to pop over with me right now and I'll introduce you to them? I know you've already met Mavis, Aunt Gus, but she may not remember you."

Gus, sensing an opportunity to get one up on Amanda said airily, "Oh, Mavis and I know each other. I went up to see her with Marion a few times when she was in Calgary, you know." Actually, the "few" was exactly twice and that had only happened because Gus had not been able to come up with effective reasons *not* to go on a couple of occasions when Marion had caught her by surprise.

This revelation did not have the desired effect, however, because Amanda had already jumped up saying, "Okay, let's *go.*" Claire snickered silently to herself. She could see that this proposed cohabitation between the two of them was going to be very interesting!

The meeting went very well. Amanda complimented Mavis on her pleasant smile and, having ascertained that the assistant, Janelle, knew how to play Canasta, went home to get a couple of decks of cards. By the time Claire left, the three of them were sitting around the dining room table engaged in a game and Mavis' chair had been pulled up so she could watch and participate in her own way. Gus enjoyed card games and she liked the idea of playing cards with the younger assistant since she had an aversion to being seen as old. Hence, she was beginning to see some possible advantages to this arrangement.

Claire returned home at that point and contemplated her next task which might not be so easy to negotiate. She was beginning to feel like she had undertaken the labors of Hercules. Having attained Jimmy's permission and the necessary contact information in advance, she sat down at her desk and phoned Moira's daughter, Carla. Claire had been asking Jimmy to do this for the past several days but he kept putting it off so Claire finally agreed to take it on. Since she'd not been directly involved in Moira's apprehension and was in fact unknown to Carla, she could not imagine there would be any hard feelings directed against her. As it happened, Carla responded that she was quite anxious to sell the house but had thought it would be necessary to do some renovations first before putting it on the market. Claire then explained who would be living in the house and the significant and unique renovations that would need to be made. And even further renovations would likely be necessary once Mavis and Bill had moved in and their needs could be better assessed. Thus, it would not be suitable to buy a house that had just been renovated. Carla, instead of being resistant to this arrangement, seemed surprisingly eager to meet with Claire as soon as possible. She even blurted out that the prospect of unloading the house quickly and forgetting all about it would be a great relief since it just triggered unhappy memories for her. And she arranged to meet with Claire at Moira's home that very afternoon!

Chapter 30—Striking a Deal

The Canasta game was just finishing and the three ladies were planning a second round when Claire arrived and interrupted. "I need Mavis to come with me to Moira's house. Her daughter will be meeting me there in half an hour. "Janelle, can you find a nice top for her? She's spilled some of her breakfast on this one, I see. Then can you help me back her down the steps? Aunt Gus and Amanda, do you think you could just brace the chair from the front so it does not come down too fast? Would that be too hard on you?" As soon as she said this, Claire could have bitten her tongue. She knew how sensitive Aunt Gus was about any suggestion that she was getting on in years. However, Amanda responded quickly that she would be happy to do it and of course Gus agreed, not to be outdone.

Naturally, both of them were full of questions about why Claire was meeting with Carla but she simply said she would tell them later and right now she needed to hurry. Claire was remembering that Moira's house had a patio door almost on grade level and she could probably get her through that quite easily. It would have been the easiest way to get her out of Jimmy's house as well but the trouble is it was quite thoroughly blocked at this point with all Mavis's extra paraphernalia.

It was tight but Claire managed to get Mavis over to Moira's house just a couple of minutes after Carla pulled up. It was never a quick or easy process getting people like Jessie and Mavis ready to go anywhere. Mavis seemed excited to be going out and had a big smile on her face when she was introduced to Carla. Carla greeted her pleasantly enough but with a quizzical look. Claire explained that Jimmy had moved his sister up and she was helping out just until he could get all the proper arrangements in place. She just hoped that her snoopy aunt would not come dragging over with Janelle since she was trying to score some sympathy points.

They brought Mavis in and she seemed to be excited to see a new place. Claire talked to her constantly for reassurance and also to role model to Carla that there was a real person there who needed and deserved to be treated as such. Mavis made it pretty clear that she was feeling quite comfortable with Claire.

They toured the house together and Claire asked if Carla would stay with Mavis while she checked out the basement on her own. She noted that it was warm and dry with basement windows large enough to crawl through in case of fire. There was also a two piece bath and a separate shower stall. A fairly new looking washer and drier were installed as was a good sized laundry sink. Now she just had to see if and what she could negotiate with Carla.

When she went upstairs, Claire found that Carla had wheeled Mavis into the kitchen and was making tea, talking away quietly to her all the time. At Claire's look of surprise and appreciation, Carla responded, "My Aunt Jane, my dad's sister, had a massive stroke in her fifties. After that, she was wheelchair bound and she could not talk. Aunt Jane never married so she lived with us for a while until my mother made arrangements to put her in an institution. Mom really resented having her around. Anyway, while Aunt Jane was living with us, which was about five months, I got in the habit of talking to her all the time even though she could not answer back. I always liked Aunt Jane."

"What happened to her?" Claire asked.

"She died a few months after she went into the institution. Dad always said she had nothing left to live for. She was a proud and independent woman who had made her own way all her life and the thought of being completely dependent on strangers for everything was just too much for her. I don't think my father ever forgave my mother for pushing her out."

"What happened to your father?" Claire asked.

"Well, I was still a teenager when all this happened but, after I moved out on my own a few years later to do my Commerce degree at Simon Fraser University in Vancouver. I never returned home. Shortly after I left, my Dad left, too. They never seemed very close or happy with each other when I was growing up."

"And where is he now?"

"He died five years ago of a massive heart attack. He lived alone and the postman discovered him a few days later. He noted all the mail and newspapers stacking up and peeked through the window and saw him stretched out on the floor." Carla paused for a moment and then added in a sad voice, "I still feel very bad about that. I had been meaning to call him that whole week but I was very busy at work and it just kept slipping my mind."

Claire nodded sympathetically. "And now your mother is in prison under a life sentence. That must be very hard on you. And it's probably hard to think of getting rid of your childhood home. Are you sure you are ready to do that, that you won't have any regrets?"

"Believe me, growing up as an only child with an angry and overbearing mother and a sad, weak father, did not leave me with any fond attachment to my childhood home. I'm ready!"

Claire hesitated a moment, deciding how to delicately phrase her next concern. "Well, technically I suppose the house still belongs to your mother. Do you think she'll be willing to sign the sales agreement?"

"Oh, I got power of attorney when she went to prison. She had to give it to me so I could handle her business affairs. She has already signed an agreement leaving me half the profits. The rest are to be put in trust for her just in case she ever gets out or has some other use for the money."

"Well, then, I guess that brings us to the business part," Claire said. "How much were you thinking of asking?"

"Carla looked at her shrewdly and then said, "According to the professionals I have talked to it's worth about $300,000.00."

Claire quailed inwardly but then pulled herself together. This was important and she could not be weak. "That's very different from the figure I had in mind. I guess I'd need to have a house inspector evaluate it before I could negotiate anything. I can see myself that it appears to have the original furnace and wiring and probably is not up to code. If an inspector comes out he'll probably note all sorts of problems and demand that they be fixed before you sell it."

"What price were you thinking then?" Carla asked nervously.

"Well, I've done some renovations and heard a lot about them through the years in my professional work as an interior decorator. From what I can gather, houses of this age and in this kind of condition and in this type of neighborhood are going for as little as $175,000.00."

"That's ridiculous!" Carla retorted angrily.

"Well, ridiculous or not," Claire replied smoothly, "we've been looking around and we know that is possible. Our price range is fairly narrow because it's based on whatever money parents have been able to put in trust for the three young people involved." After a pause, she added, "We have actually seen houses in better shape than this selling in that range so...I don't know." She paused again and then said, "Of course, our special interest in this particular house is its location. We want to build a strong community around Mavis and her two housemates and that will be easier to do with Mavis's brother right across the street." Claire paused again and then added reflectively, "But maybe I've been looking at this all wrong. Roscoe's father—Roscoe is going to be the third room-mate—is looking to buy a house for him and his wife. In one area we looked there were several possible houses for sale. Maybe he and Jimmy could move there. Maybe Jimmy would like to sell his own house anyway. It must be pretty painful to stay there after his wife was murdered right in the living room."

Carla winced when Claire said this, remembering who was responsible for that murder. She sighed and said, "I know the house needs some work and I really don't want to get into it. I guess I can bring the price down to 275 but I still say 175 is utterly ridiculous. You just have to read the paper and you know three bedroom homes in Edmonton are worth more than that. The prices have been going up for years!"

"Yes, but when you read those articles you see they are talking about average houses. I'm afraid this house is somewhat below average at the moment," Claire replied. She paused and then added, "But I do see your point. Naturally, you want to get everything you can for it. I guess if you put it in the hands of an agent you might get more...of course you'd have to pay the real estate fee, 7%, I think. And, if I recall, there was a picture of the house on the news when the murder happened. Some people might be put off by that." Claire paused again. "I guess this all must be very difficult for you," she said, sympathetically. "I'm pretty sure I could offer $200,000, if that helps and if we could have immediate possession."

Carla looked at her hopefully. "I can't do that…but maybe $250,000?"

Claire shook her head regretfully, turned and started pushing Mavis purposefully towards the door. "Wait!" Carla said. "You must know it is worth more than 200!"

Claire turned around. "Perhaps it is," Claire said. "But for us, it's also a matter of what these people, who have no possibility of working for enough money to pay a mortgage, can spend. Again she paused. "Maybe I can chip in some money and get others to do the same. Maybe somehow we could raise $225,000. But even if we could do that, and I'd have to talk to some people before promising, there's absolutely no way we could do more—and we could only do that if the sale was private and did not involve any building inspectors who would demand renovations we would not be able to afford right away. Would you consider that?" As Claire said this she was busy putting Mavis's coat on preparatory to leaving. Mavis suddenly turned towards Carla and gave her a big smile!

Carla involuntarily smiled back. Then she turned to Claire and said, "I'll have to go home and think about it and check with some people. When do you think you will know if you can make that offer from your end?"

"I should be able to get an answer in a couple of days," Claire said soberly. She added wistfully, "It would be so nice to have Mavis here where Jimmy could pop by and see her every day—and I only live about ten blocks away, myself. I hope we can work something out but we can only do what we can do."

They parted then, both with their own private mixed feelings of shame and excited anticipation. Claire felt like a mean bully, grinding Carla down remorselessly when she already had such a burden to carry with a mother as a murderer. Carla felt somehow vaguely responsible for what her mother had done to deprive Jimmy of his wife and Mavis of somebody who could have been a sisterly support to her. She, of course, was unaware of the spousal and sister-in-law relationships that had actually existed!

Chapter 31—Building a Castle in the Sand?

After resettling Mavis at home with the assistant, Claire checked her watch. Two o'clock. She phoned Dan, who was working at home and made sure that he would be there when Jessie arrived at 3:15 on the school bus, just in case the unreliable Amy did not show up. He wanted to know what Claire needed to do so urgently but she just vaguely implied that it was business related.

The next three hours were spent visiting Marion at the hospital and Fuji and his wife, Yuna, at their son's home. Actually, Roscoe's father had been named Fukashi but he'd shortened it to Fuji because it was easier for Canadians to pronounce and remember since most people had heard of the famous Mount Fuji in Japan. After explaining the proposed price agreement on Moira's house, Claire then had the delicate task of asking the respective guardians about the financial resources of Bill and Roscoe.

Marion told Claire that Bill had about $55,000 in trust. "His parents died when they were still fairly young and they didn't have that much invested in their home and no other resources to speak of. They left him about $35,000.00 and with my late husband's assistance I was able to invest it wisely. The market was pretty good until a few years ago and I've always kept it in safe funds so we did not lose out for him during the crash. And I could add the extra to balance out his share. I have some small investments which Hilda does not know about. But the thing is Hilda is Bill's beneficiary. She got me to get a will set up for him—said otherwise the government might get all that money when he died. Would you be able to set up the house sale so she gets Bill's share if something happens to him?"

Claire bit down hard on the inside of her lip to keep from saying something she shouldn't. Instead she replied, "Marion, could you excuse me for a few minutes? I really need to use the washroom. I've been running around all day!" With that, Claire rushed off and from the privacy of a stall called Tia. Tia always knew what to say. But Claire was so upset she had problems even hearing Tia over the phone.

Finally, Tia convinced her to calm down and told her how to best handle it. Claire returned to Marion with a smile on her face and said blandly, "Now, where were we?" Marion repeated her request and Claire responded as Tia had coached her. "Generally in the case of a joint mortgage the surviving mortgagees automatically inherit. But I'm sure that would not be a problem for Hilda. She just did not want the government to get the money but I'm sure she would not want Jimmy's friends to have to sell their home if something happened to him?"

"Marion responded slowly. "Ye-e-s, that makes sense. But I just hope I can convince Hilda. She's likely to get pretty upset when she hears."

Claire bit her lip but did not respond directly. Instead she said, "Well, I'm going off to talk to Roscoe's parents and then to Jimmy. I'll see what they have to say."

Roscoe's parents assured Claire that Roscoe could provide his share since their house in Calgary had just been sold. They were quite willing to make the other two buyers to the new house, Roscoe's beneficiaries but only if both of the other guardians agreed to that arrangement as well. Jimmy felt the same. Claire phoned Marion back with the news and Marion said she would talk to Hilda that evening. At eight, she called Claire back to say that Hilda agreed that Bill could enter into the house deal with the co-owners listed as beneficiaries to it but wanted his original will to be kept as it stood in case he died with other assets or even if he turned out to be the last surviving partner in the house because if that happened and he predeceased Hilda she would then inherit the house. Claire spent a further hour after that venting to Tia on the phone about greed, opportunism and exploiting vulnerable people. But all Tia would say was, "It's dangerous to judge others. You never know what motivates people to think and do the things they do."

The next day, Claire got back to Carla to let her know that the buyers could proceed with an offer of $225,000 if they could take possession on the first of February which was the coming week. Carla had talked to a few people and better appreciated the complications which would arise if a building inspector was called in and she had also discovered that there were similar houses in this price range, although not many. This was definitely a bottom end deal for her. However, she accepted it grudgingly, just wanting to get it settled and done with at this point.

Chapter 32—What about Staff?

Claire had also been busy exploring agencies but none that she heard good things about were interested and others she'd heard about were too small, too new or too iffy to consider. When she reported this to PDD, they recommended that the three families proceed with a "family-managed" model for the time being until other issues were resolved and they could either find an appropriate agency or pursue agency status themselves. "Family-managed" was a new model the Edmonton PDD had introduced to provide funding support for staffing for those families unwilling to let go of the care of their adult children. They were able to operate much like an agency with some administrative support for handling payroll and other office matters and were free, within certain parameters, to hire the people they felt could best support their loved ones.

Claire arranged a meeting with all the guardians for the next evening at Jimmy's house and pitched the idea of a "family managed" program. "I know something about the adult world in Edmonton from some of my friends whose children are part of it and I know what I am wanting for Jessie. I'd like to see the same thing for Mavis and Bill and Roscoe. I'd like us to have control over hiring staff and developing the best programs for them so they can enjoy their lives more."

"It still seems like a lot of work. And none of us really know anything about it. How could we manage?" Jimmy asked.

"I know people who are doing it," said Claire. "I could help." But even as she said it, she could hear Dan's voice telling her not to get involved. "And we can still set up an informal board of interested people to act as advisors. I talked to Bess at the hospital already about this idea and she's willing to get involved as a board member."

"What about the payroll and the accounts? Who would take that on?" Jimmy asked. The funder will want annual financial reports. That could get pretty complicated."

At this point, the whole group was looking excited, caught up in imagining the possibilities and how much this system could do to make all their lives better: less worry for them and more freedom and enjoyment in life for Mavis, Roscoe and Bill. Marion suddenly spoke up with uncharacteristic forcefulness. "Hilda is an accountant and I don't see why she couldn't take care of the books. It's about time she did something for her cousin. As a matter of fact, I'm going to tell her that if she does not agree to sit on this board and help out *and* do the books I'm going to change my will and leave Bill the proceeds from the house. *That* will bring her around pretty fast because if there's one thing that Hilda and that husband of hers love it's money!"

The rest of them looked at Marion in amazement. Nobody had ever heard her talk that way before! Claire felt an electric tingle down her spine. Something wonderful was happening before her eyes. They were now all in this together and she no longer had to carry the burden of her schemes and plans for the three adults locked inside her head!

Chapter 33—Claire Hatches Another Plot

Bill had now been in the hospital almost a month. He seemed to be increasingly depressed and withdrawn, almost robotic in his responses. He did not even get that excited when Mavis came to visit about twice a week. Marion continued to sit with him by the hour but he increasingly ignored her, playing either with his Gameboy or else just rocking silently back and forth. He made no effort to communicate with any of the others there, ignoring them when possible and actively avoiding the ones who tried to initiate contact with him. When Marion talked to Claire about it, she just shook her head sorrowfully, blaming herself over and over for bringing Bill to Edmonton in the first place. "None of this would have happened if only...." she always started out. Claire worried even more than Marion because she saw the anger just below the surface in Bill that bubbled up periodically between his bouts of lethargy. She'd been very busy with the guardianship and trusteeship issues, the house purchase and helping the families negotiate with AADL for necessary equipment and PDD for necessary staffing support. She could hardly do more and was increasingly resenting Tia's lack of progress in searching out a viable murder suspect. She arranged a meeting with her that evening, feeling, for the first time coolness toward this person she'd come to think of as her closest friend.

Claire was vaguely surprised when she walked into Tia's house at nine that evening, after both Mario and Jessie were asleep for the night. There was some slight clutter about, and was that a sheen of dust she saw on the reception table in the front hall? Tia greeted her in her night clothes with a short cotton dressing gown over top. Coffee was waiting but the cake which accompanied it was cold from the fridge and several days old. Tia looked very tired.

"What is going on, Tia?" Claire asked without preamble. "You look exhausted!"

"Extra shifts at the Centre," Tia replied tersely. "One of the cleaning staff for the Human Resources office got married and has taken a month off. I've been covering for her for the last two weeks. Her shifts are afternoon ones, 3 to 9, and one of the days, Wednesday, is the same one as my morning shift so I don't get much of a break on that day. She works Tuesday, Wednesday and Thursday and, as you know, I do Monday, Wednesday and Friday—and tomorrow is Wednesday. That's the evening I clean the administrative, professional and human resources offices, so we'll have to make this short."

"What about Mario? Why did you ever take this on, Tia?"

"My neighbor keeps Mario at her house until I get home and I don't know why I agreed to do it—because they asked me, I guess."

"Remind me why you're there again?" Claire asked caustically.

"I know," Tia said. "But there's so much need."

"And Bill's need? And Marion's need?" Tia did not respond. Claire stopped talking suddenly. "Wait a minute! You say you'll be working in the Human Resources office? That won't be staffed like the client units. They won't have staff in there at night. Is that correct?"

"Yes, I can't remember seeing anybody in any of those offices on that floor after six, except occasionally the security guard making his rounds."

"Does he follow a regular schedule?"

"He's generally there about half past the hour so I guess it takes him about an hour to go through the whole center."

"Do you still have your cousin's lock picks?

"Ye-e-s. Why?"

"According to you, the only possible connection you have been able to uncover is that both Annette and this Frankie Jessick person come from Barbados. We need to find out if Richards is Annette's maiden name or her married name and what her maiden name was. We also need the home addresses for both her and Jessick—here and in Barbados. All that information should be in their personnel files. Have you seen any locked file cabinets in that office?"

"Yes, but I don't see how…."

"You managed with Megan's file cabinet when you were looking for *her* murderer."

"That was different. There was less likelihood of getting caught. I only had Jimmy to worry about. What if I get caught?"

"What's the worst thing that can happen? They fire you?"

"Well, all I really have is my reputation. My boss is very pleased with my work and I've already had one promotion in this short time, as you know. I'd hate for them to think badly of me."

"How about what people are thinking about Bill, Tia? And what it's doing to *his* life? Get a grip! This *is* only a *cleaning* job."

"You might not think that's so trivial if you ever end up in the hospital and get some anti-biotic resistant infection because some slob doesn't bother to clean the corners or wipe down the door handles!"

"Look, I know it's important and I really admire the way you clean. But right now I think Bill's life is *more* important. Also, can I remind you that you did not even *want* to take this job; I had to talk you *into* it! Besides, if you plan it around the security guard's schedule you probably won't get caught."

"Okay," Tia said resignedly. "I'll try tomorrow. There's a five-drawer lateral file cabinet that I've seen the head of personnel open up to file something in. I will try there first."

"Good! And before you dig out the lock picks, check the desk drawers, especially the middle one. People try to keep things simple and I've observed in different offices people reaching into that pen tray you often find in those shallow middle drawers to fish out file cabinet keys."

Chapter 34—You Win Some and You Lose Some

The next afternoon found Tia cleaning furiously in order to finish her work early. She skipped supper and her regular coffee break time and by 8:45, she was through, just as the security guard left the floor to carry on his surveillance elsewhere. Tia quietly entered the Human Resources office and closed the door behind her. She shuffled quickly through all the drawers she could open in the three desks in the room with no luck. The middle drawer of one desk was locked. She pondered briefly trying to pick that lock or working directly on the file cabinet. The desk faced the door but if she worked at the cabinet her back would be to the door. Also at the desk she could sit down and she was very tired. Tia worked away trying not to leave any telltale scratches on the lock and in 10 minutes she had it open and found a ring of small keys that looked like file cabinet keys. She must be developing criminal expertise, Tia thought sourly.

Tia checked her watch. It was already nine o'clock. She opened the door but apart from the hall lights the offices were dark and she heard nothing. Quickly she tried the keys and the third one worked on the lateral file cabinet. The first drawer held brochures, work plans and bulletins but the second drawer looked promising. The files were arranged alphabetically and she scanned quickly through to the *J*'s but found no Jessick there. A furtive check of her watch revealed that it was already 10 minutes after the hour. Tia could feel the sweat on her forehead and between her shoulder blades. Then she saw what she should have noticed to begin with, a small card in the name plate outside the drawer labeled 'administrative personnel.' She scanned the drawers and the 4th drawer was labeled *nursing*. She quickly found *Jessick* and *Richards*, removed the files and closed the drawer. Just then she heard the elevator ding. The key was still in the lock and she gave it a quick turn and returned it to the desk drawer, shoved the files under the desk blotter and grabbed her dust rag just as the door opened.

"Oh, it's *you*," the security guard said. "I saw the light. Why did you close the door? You don't, usually."

"I...it was just so quiet tonight that I felt spooked. I did not feel like cleaning with my back to an open door."

"O-oh," the security guard said with what sounded to Tia like a note of doubt in his voice. "Well, I better get on," he said, and left, carefully leaving the door open behind him.

Tia did not dare to close it but she went into the attached washroom with the files and hastily photographed them with her cell phone. As she came out, she heard the elevator ding and peeped out the office door just in time to see the back of the security guard disappearing into it. Tia quickly returned the files to their proper places and locked the cabinet. Then she returned the keys but could not lock the desk drawer. She would just have to leave it unlocked and hope that whoever used that desk would think it was his or her oversight. It was just 9:35 but Tia put away her cleaning supplies and left early. Once in her car she locked all the doors and just sat there shaking for about five minutes before she felt composed enough to drive safely.

The next day, Friday, Tia called in sick. She *was* rather sick, actually, from emotional exhaustion. But more than that, she felt like a traitor and did not think she could face those people. She had already emailed the pictures she'd taken to Claire. Let Claire do the rest of the dirty work. Tia did not have the heart for it.

Claire came over at one o'clock, as they had arranged. She was carrying her briefcase and disgorged a sheaf of papers on Tia's dining room table. They were blow-ups of the files Tia had sent. Together, they studied them. "Well, it's true what my friend told me," Tia exclaimed. "Frank Jessick *does* live on the other side of the island from where Annette Richards came from."

"Yes, but Barbados is only 34 kilometres long and 23 kilometres wide at its widest point, which is where St. John parish is. Its total population as of 2012 was estimated to be 287,000. Edmonton alone has almost three times as many people and 23 kilometres is the distance from Southgate Shopping Centre to the airport. Nobody would consider that a long haul."

Tia was paying attention to Claire but at the same time browsing through Frank Jessick's file. *"Look!"* she said suddenly. It says here that Frank had an older brother who was a student at Cave Hill Medical School when he died suddenly three years ago. Isn't that where Annette Richards did her nurses' training?"

Claire was flicking rapidly through the pages laid out in front of them even as Tia was speaking. *"Yes!"* And it says here that she had just completed nurses' training when she left for Canada 2½ years ago, so that means they were probably students at the same time!"

"Should we tell Sergeant Crombie?" Tia asked. "This is definitely a connection. Maybe he can convince McCoy to follow it up."

"No. He won't think it matters. We're going to have to do this ourselves. Can you talk to your friend, Denise, and get some more information about those two schools? By the way, where does it say that Frank got his nursing assistant training? Have you found that amongst his file notes yet?"

"Hmm," Tia replied. "It says here that he completed an eleven-month vocational nursing program at Barbados Community College. That's also in St. Michael parish, just five miles outside of Bridgetown."

"When did he finish it?"

"It says here two years ago."

"Didn't you say that your friend, Denise, at work, told you that Jessick was planning to leave soon?"

"Yes, he's just staying another month to complete his Foreign Workers commitment so the center will have to pay his fare back."

"Then we have no time to lose. You better put in your notice on Monday just in case we can find a quick flight. Is a week's notice enough?"

"What do you *mean* put in my notice? I'm just getting going there!"

"Tia, I don't see what more you can do there in terms of finding Annette's killer. And what I have not had a chance to tell you is that we sealed the deal on the house today—got it for $225,000," Claire added with a note of triumph in her voice.

"Wow!"

"Yup. I could almost feel guilty except when I remember that the owner killed Megan. You can consider the low price as civil suit compensation. Besides, it's going to take a lot of work to get it ready for the three new owners."

"Three?"

"Yes. Roscoe's father is great. Bill and Mavis and Roscoe were each able to put in $60,000.00 so they are only carrying a $45,000.00 mortgage. It took some finagling at the bank to get the manager to accept their combined monthly AISH payments as a guaranteed source of income but he could not argue much because there's more money in the house than they are actually borrowing so it's a secure investment."

"Gee, it's such a small mortgage, it's kind of a shame they could not have bought the house outright."

"No, it's better this way. The interest rates are very low right now and this way they build up a credit rating just in case they ever need it. Besides, you are not taking into account closing fees and moving expenses––hook-up charges, for example. And then there are all the renovations that have to be done. Even with Jimmy and Fuji and his brother doing a lot of the work, they will still cost at least $20,000.00.

"When do you think the house will be ready?"

"Jimmy figures they can have everything done that is necessary for them to move in in a couple of weeks. He's planning to take next week off work and the other two men are retired so they are available anytime. They were down at the lumberyard already today ordering the material for a ramp and for a base in order to raise the tub and the plumber is coming late next week to hook it up."

"What about the funding?"

"I've been working on it. I've checked it out with PDD and the person I talked to suggested we proceed as a "family-managed" operation." Claire then explained what that was.

"When were you planning to tell the rest of us?"

"Don't be like that, Tia! There just has not been any time for niceties. Everything is happening at once and if we don't move fast this whole house of cards is going to fall down around our ears!"

"When do you see this all happening, then?"

"As soon as we get back from Barbados."

"What do you mean? Who's going to Barbados?"

"We are—you and me."

"No. I can't. There is my job—and what about Mario?"

"That's why I asked you to put in your resignation on Monday, Tia. And I already called your parents to see if they could come into the city for a week to look after Mario. They called me back to say their neighbor has agreed to look after their house and dog so they're good to go!"

"You know, Claire, an uncharitable person would call you 'officious!' If you're so gung-ho on this idea why don't you just go with Dan instead?"

"First of all, you know I could never get anyone to look after Jessie that long and secondly you know that Dan would never support me trying to chase down a murderer!"

Tia's head was buzzing and she hardly knew what to ask next. "What about PDD approval? It's all very well to buy a house and register an agency but there's no guarantee if or when you're going to get the government funding to cover this scheme."

"Well, as a matter of fact I've already been working on that," Claire said smugly. I've arranged a meeting next week with the intake worker and Jimmy and Marion and Fuji. The files for Mavis and Bill are already under review there and Roscoe's case should not require much scrutiny since he's coming from an institution. All three of them are high needs so I imagine they'll have to give us pretty decent funding support."

"How much is this little jaunt to Barbados going to cost? *I* don't have that kind of money!"

"I'm also working on that so don't worry about it."

Tia just shook her head and shortly after that they said good night.

Chapter 35—Salmon Swim Upstream—and So Does Claire

As she often did when finding herself in impossibly complicated situations, the next morning Claire put her head down and tackled one problem at a time. The problems, as she saw them were: getting enough money for the trip, convincing her husband, Dan, that the trip was necessary without revealing her true purpose since he was very opposed to her sleuthing, convincing Tia that she needed to come along, and figuring out what to do that could be of any possible use if and when they finally got to Barbados.

Money was first so the top of Claire's agenda was to visit Marion who, as usual, was at the hospital that day. When faced with many problems, Claire found it helpful to look at the bright side. At least, this meant that Marion's money-obsessed daughter would not be there to interfere. Also, they could talk freely in front of Bill without the likelihood of him spilling the beans!

Marion was happy to see Claire and even Bill seemed vaguely pleased. The three of them settled down together in a quiet corner of the patient lounge. Claire quickly updated Marion on all that had been happening and Marion was predictably pleased. Claire explained what Tia had accomplished in her time at the hospital, carefully lowering her voice when she described the break-in, and Marion laughed at Tia's boldness and ingenuity. Then Claire grew very serious. "This connection to Frank Jessick is the only slender link to Annette we have been able to uncover and it's not enough to take to the police, particularly McCoy, and expect them to follow up on it. As I see it we have only one possible option left in terms of advancing the investigation. Tia and I will have to go to Barbados."

"But what about her work at the Clive Centre?"

"She's putting in her letter of resignation on Monday. There's nothing more she can accomplish there in terms of the investigation. She has made one friend, Denise, who she hopes will keep her informed if anything new that is of interest emerges. We also know that Frank Jessick has resigned and is planning to leave the center at the end of the month and return to Barbados so time is of the essence."

"What can I do to help?"

"Money," Claire said simply. "I will have enough trouble convincing Dan that I need to go while not acknowledging that I am sleuthing without taking $3000.00 from the family budget—and that's the least it will cost for both of us to go. Tia certainly can't afford to chip in much."

"I can do that," Marion said. "I have three times that much in my bank account and Hilda does not know how much I have. And I also have investments I could access if I needed to. Do you think you'll need more? I can give you four?"

"No, I thought about this. It's *your* nephew we are talking about but we have all agreed to support him. Tia and I will come up with the rest."

"How will you explain your funding source to Dan without mentioning Bill?"

Claire sighed. "I promised after our last adventure that I would not lie to my husband again but life is so complicated. I think I'll just say something like this. I'm very tired. I've always wanted to see Barbados for some reason. Dan goes away on his business trips and leaves me alone with Jessie and I think it's my turn to have a break. He has one big project pending but has not received final approval on it so he has time to care for Jessie right now. All of this is true except maybe for the part about the special interest in Barbados so it isn't the worst lie I could tell," Claire added, trying to convince herself.

"It sounds plausible," Marion said, although Claire detected a small note of doubt in her voice. "I have my check book with me and I'll write you a check right now so at least you have that part off your mind."

"Does Hilda ever see your check book? Won't she have questions about that?"

"Look, Claire, you have been incredibly helpful to me and to Bill throughout this whole ordeal—which is a lot more than I can say for Hilda. I'll just tell her that I don't know how much time I have left, which is quite true, and that I wanted to do something back for you. You had talked about this holiday but did not feel you could afford it right now so I decided to make it happen."

"Okay, that sounds pretty reasonable and that's also what I'll tell Dan. Just make sure Hilda knows I did not ask for the money...which of course I did," Claire added as an after-thought.

"Don't worry. I have already thought about that because that would be the first thing Hilda would ask!"

After a brief mental struggle between curiosity and decorum, which decorum, as usual, lost, Claire asked, "Why is she that way, Marion, so worried about money? *You* are not like that and, from what I understand, Hilda and her husband are not exactly poor!"

Marion sighed. "I know she is my daughter so of course I'm biased but I really believe that Hilda, underneath everything, is a good person. Her father was very worried about money and did very well financially so he left me comfortably well off. I have of course left the proceeds from my house and everything in it to Hilda because she would expect that. However, I've named Bill as the beneficiary on a number of my investments and I also named the Forbes Center on one of them worth about $20,000.00. I figured my investments and the profits I've made because of friends who helped me to grow them since Mike died are my business and I can do what I like with them."

Marion paused for a minute and then went on. "Mike was always talking about money when Hilda was growing up. If an investment went down, which they invariably do from time to time, it was the end of the world. He created a lot of anxiety around money even though we never really wanted for anything."

"But what about Hilda? Why is *she* like that?"

"Well, all I can think is that it rubbed off on her. And then she turned around and married somebody who is the same with the same anxiety. Both Tom and Mike have rags to riches stories in their family backgrounds so maybe that's why they're the way they are—or were, in Mike's case."

"So you are saying that Hilda just got caught up in this money box and never thought to think outside it? They don't have children. They just work from what you have told me. So that should have given her plenty of time to think about what else there is to life?"

"Well, there's something else you don't know. Hilda was married to somebody else before Tom—Albert Lesore. We call him the Lesore loser. She was only 19 but insisted she was ready to marry and all she wanted at that point was to set up housekeeping and become the perfect wife and mother. Mike cashed in an investment and gave them $30,000.00 for a down payment on a three-bedroom bungalow not too far from us. All they had to do was make the payments. She left that part of it to Albert because, as she explained to us at the time, she wanted him to feel like it was his house, too. Well, Albert made the payments and when any correspondence came from the bank he read it and looked after it—or so we thought. What happened was this. Albert was never much of a worker so even though he went out the door to work every day we did not realize until the Bailiff came and foreclosed on the house and took some of the nice furniture Hilda had been collecting that Albert had actually not been working for about six months and he'd let the house payments lapse even before that. So Hilda lost the home she had set up so carefully along with her little dream of being the perfect mistress of a perfect home. And then to top it off she found out she was pregnant. But Albert convinced her they could not possibly afford to have a child and he arranged an abortion for her. They weren't legal then and in fact Hilda was four months along when she finally told him. Well,"—and here Marion broke down a little—"it turned out that this guy was quite the butcher. He got rid of the child alright but he did it in such a way that Hilda was never able to have children again. After that she just left that loser, Albert, and got a divorce and when she met Tom she did not tell him that she was sterile. However, he confessed to her that he did not really want children. The financial repercussions would just make him too anxious and he already had enough problems with anxiety. So they've been married seven years now and seem happy enough together—but I know that Hilda feels the loss of children every day. I guess that's what has made her kind of mean and suspicious and money-grabbing but I don't know what to do about it." Marion sighed again.

"Wow," Claire said. "It just goes to prove that old adage, doesn't it? Never judge a book by its cover."

Marion smiled at her gratefully.

Chapter 36—It Is Better to Tell the Truth Than to Lie

Claire was home from the hospital by one pm and Dan had still not had his lunch, so she prepared it and they sat down together. They always cherished these times alone with Jessie at school and no worker in the house. It felt almost like a date, they were so used to their life being controlled by others. After lunch they took their coffee to the main floor living room—the one they hardly ever used when the assistants were there— and sat down together for a visit uninterrupted by the needs of others.

"There's something I need to talk to you about," Claire said rather assertively.

Dan braced himself because when Claire used that particular tone of voice he'd learned to expect the worst. "Ye-e-s?" he asked cautiously.

"I'm tired. I want a holiday and we can't go together because of Jessie. So I want to go to Barbados with Tia," Claire blurted.

"Why Barbados?" Dan asked in a deceptively mild tone.

"Oh, I just think it must be an interesting country, away out there in the Atlantic away from everything else and yet with one of the highest literacy rates in the world!"

"And?" he prompted, "Don't I recall that the suspected murderer of that nurse, at least the one *you* suspect, comes from Barbados?"

Claire gritted her teeth. She really must learn not to share so much with Dan. "Okay, fine," she said. "Maybe there's a second reason."

"First is more what you mean," Dan interjected sotto voce.

"But my other point still stands. The fact is you get away a lot more than I do!"

"For business!" he said firmly.

"Well, this is business, too! Bill's whole future is at stake—and this is *killing* Marion!"

"And if you keep sticking your nose into what is not *your* business, one of these days it will kill *you*!"

"Ah, but this time is different," Claire retorted. "There's no way I can approach anybody in his family to find out what happened to his brother or what his or his brother's connection might have been with Annette because they'll tell Frank and he's already leaving for Barbados in three weeks and then he'll just bolt sooner. So this has to be handled very discreetly—maybe some library research, maybe a trip to the nursing schools they attended, nothing more. And I *am* interested in Barbados."

"What about money?" Dan asked. "Barbados is a long way from here and airfare is bound to be expensive. I know you need a holiday but what's wrong with a week in Mexico on the beach?"

"Marion insisted on paying for it. She's desperate to get some answers and can't go herself, even if her heart wasn't so bad that she would never get insurance. She just can't leave Bill alone. But I did refuse to take more than $3000.00 from her. I said that Tia and I could manage the rest and we had a commitment to Bill, too, at this point." Claire crossed her fingers behind her back to cancel out her selective rendering of the truth.

Dan gazed steadily at Claire and she squirmed slightly but decided that any further embellishments would be self-defeating. The time for silence had come.

"Well, Claire, I can't deny that you both need and deserve a change of scene. But I hope you're not holding anything back about a possible danger element. Remember, you have a responsibility to be around for Jessie—*and* for me."

"Thank you, Dan. Thank you for understanding," Claire said simply, and she kissed him lightly on the mouth. "I'm going out for a while. I should be back before it's time for Jessie's supper."

Claire's next stop was to see Amanda and Aunt Gus. They were delighted to see her, brewed a pot of tea and demanded all the latest details on "the case" and on the grand scheme to set up the three new home owners in their own home. Claire told them the highlights but spent the most time explaining about Frank Jessick and about his imminent departure for Barbados. She laid down her credit card, pointing out the security code on the back and asked them to spend some time checking with Expedia and other sources for a good flight and accommodation package to Bridgetown, Barbados, for two. It needed to be no sooner than next weekend and no later than two weeks from now. Claire explained the urgency and told them if they found one they should book it immediately because the good deals never lasted. Then she left them to work on it while she went over to see Tia since it was now 3:30, meaning Tia should be home from work. It was Amanda who would find the answer, Claire knew, since she was quite computer-savvy for a lady her age, but Claire had given the card to Gus in order to include her and to allow her to save face.

Claire stopped at a bakery and picked up a decadent looking Chocolate Mousse cake for Tia but Tia was not as happy to see Claire as she usually was. It took two cups of coffee and two pieces of cake and all the explaining that could happen within that period of consumption to bring her around. Claire patiently drew it out for her—how they had no other options left and what that could ultimately mean for Bill. Finally, Tia came around. Claire said she'd find the money to cover any funding shortfall, but Tia insisted that she could contribute $500.00 because of the unexpected extra money she had been making at the hospital.

She also told Claire that she'd submitted her resignation and made the coming Friday her last regular day. However, the head of housekeeping had begged her to reconsider while she was away and to continue to come in at least on a casual basis and even as a consultant about good cleaning practices when she returned. Tia had been flattered and had agreed to consider it. Claire sighed impatiently when Tia said this but said nothing out loud. Tia went on to mention that she had had morning coffee with Denise and they had exchanged contact information, both phone and email so they could keep in touch. Denise wanted Claire and Tia to visit her family who lived at Four Roads in the St. John Parish like Frank Jessick, and Tia had agreed that if they ended up going they would certainly do that. Denise knew about the investigation but had promised to keep it to herself. Now Denise asked if she could share this information with her family so they could begin snooping around, but Tia had said no. She was afraid that something would get back to Frank, and Claire agreed that that had been a good call.

Claire was about to leave when the phone rang. It was Amanda and Tia put her on speaker. "Your tickets are booked. You leave a week from this Sunday and it is a week-long trip. A couple who booked this trip cancelled so I got it pretty cheap. You want to know how much?" Amanda crowed.

"Okay, I'll bite," said Claire.

"$1450.00 each and with tax it comes to $1602.00!"

"Fantastic!" Tia exclaimed. "What about stop-overs?"

"Just one, about three hours, in Houston."

"That's really great, Amanda—and thanks, Gus. Did you have any trouble using my card?"

"None at all. I sound young, you know. They thought I was you. I did not tell them otherwise. Why complicate things?" Gus said smugly.

Claire smirked but said nothing. After she hung up the phone, she said to Tia, "Well, that's it! We've got the money, the tickets and Dan's on our side. Nothing is going to stop us now!"

"You're forgetting one person—Jimmy. He already thinks you're a bad influence on me. He told me so!"

"Okay, Tia, if you're going to be in this relationship you better start learning some defensive manoeuvers and learn to think ahead. What are you going to say to him and what are you not going to say?" They rehearsed this for a while and then Claire left.

Chapter 37—The Storm Before the Calm

The next week was a dizzy whirl of activity for both Tia and Claire. First of all, it was not as easy to bring Jimmy around to accepting the trip as they had thought. However, more even than Dan because of his direct investment in the house, he knew that there was a serious problem to solve and they could not count on McCoy, so with many warnings and admonishments he finally conceded. Secondly, the people at the hospital were very unhappy with the prospect of Tia's departure and tried various techniques to convince her to stay including offering her the Barbados week off with pay and promising that she would never have to take on any more extra shifts. Tia was bemused and flattered by all this obvious appreciation of her cleaning talents, appreciation which had been in short supply in the past, but she was finally able to clear her head and stand firm. She knew where her primary responsibilities lay. Once the new organization was established and the three owners, as she had come to think of them, were ensconced, she would have to be the key person responsible for overseeing it and ensuring that everything ran smoothly. That meant she had to be on-site or, in her case, just across the street.

Claire's issues were even more complicated. She had to make sure all the forms were properly signed for the house financing and also that the paperwork given to them by the PDD intake worker was completed for each of the three new homeowners so that their funding applications could proceed. She also wanted to find a mature person who could become the team leader in the home in order to take the pressure off Tia and she had a nagging thought at the back of her head that from what she'd heard, maybe this Denise person could be it. She asked Tia to sound her out that last week and it turned out that Denise was interested. They would discuss it further after the trip. There were still some final details to be taken care of for the house transfer of title and she made sure that Jimmy was going to handle them. Finally, and most importantly, there were Marion and Bill. Claire had been supporting them both heavily. The situation was precarious and she enlisted Roscoe's father to bring Roscoe up for a visit at least twice and Jimmy to do the same with Mavis. She arranged for Aunt Gus to go along with Jimmy so she could visit with Marion while Bill visited with Jimmy and Mavis. She couldn't do more on that front and just hoped it was enough. Finally, and most critically, she had to organize all Jessie's special meals for the time she was away and ensure that she had adequate staffing coverage so the burden on Dan would not be too heavy. And then, minor detail, she had to shuffle a few–a very few–client appointments around.

Chapter 38—Barbados or Bust—or Both!

Claire and Tia were at the airport at 5:30 a.m. on the day of their flight, bleary-eyed and nervously reviewing what they'd remembered to bring and what they may have forgotten.

Suddenly Claire groaned. "A-a-h! I forgot my curling iron! I'm dead. I'll look like a freak all week!"

"Never mind. You can use mine," Tia said.

"Yours! What do you need a curling iron for? Just look at all those curls you have!"

"And those curls would be frizz without it! That's the trouble with you 'straights.' You think you're the only ones with problems. Believe *me*, dealing with natural curls has its challenges!"

Claire relaxed after this, chose to drink de-caf at Starbucks which, strangely enough, always served it in the morning but never in the evening, just in case she could have a nap later, and settled in to work on the *Edmonton Journal* crossword puzzle from yesterday, there no longer being a Sunday paper. Tia pulled out a delicate blouse she was crocheting for her mother for Christmas and began working on it. Claire just looked at her and thought, "Mrs. Domesticity!"

They arrived in Barbados at ten Barbadian time which was eight Alberta time. The total flight time had been 12 hours, which included a three-hour layover in Houston, Texas. Their travel package included bussing to the hotel and back and by 11:30 they were settled in their room and collapsed in bed ready to sleep the sleep of the just.

The next morning they arose with that peculiar sense of aimlessness which follows an intense period of planning and preparation in order to get to a destination where one has made no particular plans or preparation. They made themselves presentable and wandered up to the 5th floor of their hotel for their complimentary breakfast which was also part of the package. Claire saw Tia eying the various offers meaningfully and laid a cautionary hand on her arm. "No, we're not going to start surreptitiously stuffing buns and cold cuts in our purses in order to enjoy a free lunch, painful as that may be to you!"

Tia argued the point half-heartedly. "Look at all these apes, greedily taking more than they need or can even eat and then wasting it!" If we don't take some extra we won't get our share—and we paid for it!"

"We also paid for the experience of acting gentile and being looked after for a week and that's not how to go about it! And furthermore we're supposed to be having a holiday and part of that is enjoying the local culture and the local foods. Ham and buns from some undoubtedly American Costco is not it. Also, may I remind you that Gus and Amanda got us a really good deal so we can afford to loosen up a bit." Tia grudgingly conceded the point but rebelliously stuffed a couple of teabags in her purse.

After breakfast, Tia and Claire sat in the adjoining lounge with a second cup of coffee and perused the tourist brochures they'd collected on arrival. Suddenly Tia's phone rang. When she answered it, a musical voice told her that she was Denise's mother, Rosalina. Could she and her husband, Benson, pick them up and bring them back for lunch to meet their family? After passing the message on to Claire, Tia accepted for them happily and Rosalina told them that they would be pulling up in front of their hotel in about an hour and they would be driving a 1998 Honda Civic, blue gray in color.

"Now aren't you glad you don't have a purse full of buns and cold cuts to contend with?" Claire asked rhetorically. Tia did not respond. She was thinking ahead to tomorrow's breakfast and about how useful a larger purse and a couple of baggies would be!

Chapter 39—Friends in Waiting

When Rosalina and Benson pulled up in front of the hotel, they both jumped out of the car and hugged Tia and Claire warmly before even getting through the introductions. They made it clear that any friend or friend of a friend of Denise was a friend of theirs!

Tia and Claire felt quite overwhelmed by all this warmth and enthusiasm from virtual strangers. Various polite lines went through their heads about not going to any trouble or about what a nice person Denise was or about how neat and orderly and peaceful everything seemed to be in Barbados but none of them seemed quite appropriate, so they just sat in a happy daze listening quietly to Rosalina rattle on about island politics, the state of the roads and their plans for participating in the up and coming crop-over festival.

Once at the family home—a modest bungalow with an inviting courtyard and outdoor kitchen—they were introduced to Aurora, Denise's 22 year old sister. She had been preparing the mid-day meal and they soon sat down to it. Once their respective plates had been filled by the solicitous Rosalina, and over-filled in Tia's opinion, there was time to talk. Tia explained how she had come to know Denise and regaled them with stories about the cleaning challenges at the Center and how she and Denise shared the same ideas about what it meant to clean. She made a point of saying she had found no common ground on that subject with any of the other staff members because they felt it was just a job to be gotten through as quickly and minimally as possible.

They resented Tia for talking about better ways to clean. Denise, by contrast, had the kind of personality that allowed her to get along with everybody. She cleaned just as well or better than Tia but had the sense to keep her head down and not rub it in other's faces.

When Claire felt that Tia had held the spotlight long enough, she turned to Aurora and asked, "Do you have any other brothers and sisters apart from Denise?"

"I have a younger brother, Jeremy. He just finished his vocational nursing program at Unitek College and is in the process of applying for some different nursing positions at several hospitals. He's away today at an interview in Crab Hill."

"I hope he gets a job closer to home so he can continue living here," Rosalina interjected. Crab Hill is in Saint Lucy Parish about 50 kilometers from here. It was bad enough that he chose to go to Unitek to do his training and pay so much for his accommodation! If he can live at home, he can save up money. He's hoping to go back and do a full nursing degree at the University of the West Indies at their Cave Hill campus near Bridgetown and he'll need plenty of money for that.

"Why did Jeremy choose to go to Unitek College?" Claire asked, for want of something to say to keep the conversation going. "Isn't there a vocational nursing program closer to here?"

"Yes, he could have gone to Barbados Community College in Bridgetown, but he said the program was better at Unitek. If you want my opinion, I think he just wanted an excuse to live on his own!" Aurora responded.

"It was important to get solid training if he wants to get into the nursing degree program at Cave Hill, and he's been thinking of that for a long time as you know, Aurora," Rosalina responded with a touch of censure in her voice.

"Well, there *are* other nursing programs available on the island," Aurora replied. "I'm sure *one* of them would have let him in."

"Cave Hill is the best, he's been told—and you know he wants to spend a few years travelling and nursing abroad," Rosalina rejoined. "For that, good credentials are important!"

"Where does he want to travel to?" Claire asked.

"Actually, he's considering Canada—Edmonton in fact. This friend of his told him that his brother likes Edmonton. It has all the amenities of a large city but housing prices and rent are still very reasonable."

Claire got a funny tingly feeling which she recognized from past experience as a kind of prescience. "Does this friend have a name?" she asked.

"Yes—Georgie Jessick."

Tia and Claire looked at each other. "And is his brother Frank Jessick?"

"I think that's what Jeremy said," Aurora replied. "But how did *you* know?"

"Frank is the nursing attendant on that unit where Annette Richards was killed. Surely Denise told you the story?"

"Y-e-s," Rosalina interjected. "But she didn't mention any names. Well, it is a small world, isn't it—and Barbados is *very* small!"

"Did he mention why Frank went to Edmonton in the first place?" Tia asked Aurora.

"No, that's all I know," Aurora responded.

"Are we going to have a chance to meet your son, Rosalina? I'd like to report back to Denise how he's doing," Tia asked.

"He'll likely be here tomorrow. He rarely misses Sunday dinner and we'd like you to join us for that, too." After a brief pause, Rosalina added, "Why don't you just stay over instead of going back to Bridgetown tonight? We can fix you up with pajamas and toothbrushes and it will just be simpler that way. Besides, that will give us a better chance to get acquainted."

"Oh, we couldn't impose like that!" was Claire's kneejerk English response.

"Well, I'm sure you have other things you'd rather be doing. You are on holiday after all," Rosalina said stiffly.

Claire looked at Tia and Tia nodded her head ever so slightly. Claire turned to Rosalina and said, "Actually, we're not really on holiday. I think we need to tell you something,"

Chapter 40—Claire and Tia Have New Allies

Together, Claire and Tia blurted out the story of Marion and Bill and what had happened at the Clive Centre and the reason he was suspected of Annette's murder. Then they talked about the other staff on the two units and how Frank seemed to be the only one who could have any connection to her. Claire told them how upset Marion was and how she had wanted them to come here to see if there was any possible clue they could find to follow up because the police were not looking beyond Bill even though it seemed impossible that he could have done it. The story was met with a satisfying number of *oohs* and *aahs* and by the time they were through, it was clear that Rosalina, Benson and Aurora were solidly on their team and ready to do anything they could to help.

This story and the follow-up questions took up most of the evening and by the time they were through, everyone was ready for bed. Tia and Claire borrowed pajamas from Aurora, and Rosalina gave them each a new toothbrush. They were grateful to crawl into bed after such a long day and they fell asleep before exchanging more than a few words in private.

Jeremy arrived at 11:30 the next morning and was introduced to Tia and Claire who were in the kitchen learning about Barbadian cuisine and helping out where they could. Aurora was busily gutting and plucking two big chickens and Tia and Claire were keeping their heads turned studiously away. They occupied themselves with their tasks which were to slice up the onions and garlic for the Bajan baked chicken recipe Rosalina was overseeing while holding the rum bottle––the magic ingredient—at the ready.

Already, Tia and Claire could feel themselves slipping into a different frame of mind, more languorous and less stressed. Nothing seemed quite as important as it had back home. Once the chickens were safely in the oven where they would be slow-cooked into island glory along with a special Bajan rice and yam dish, Claire and Tia joined Jeremy and Aurora in the living room. They had abandoned all question of secrecy and told Jeremy all about Annette Richards' murder and their reason for being there.

Jeremy listened to the story with a shocked face and when they finished, he blurted out, "Wow! I never thought it was true! I thought he was just letting off steam. Who does that?" He looked at them with big eyes.

"Well, technically, we don't absolutely know that Frankie Jessick killed her," Claire said. "We only know that it's very unlikely that Bill did. For one thing, how would Bill get access to a carving knife from the kitchen? It's not like anyone would leave it hanging around the patient lounge or that staff would allow a patient to wander through the kitchen!"

"Well, if Frankie did kill her, I can tell you why," Jeremy said. "Frankie and Geordie had an older half-brother named Marvin Applewaite. They had the same mother—her maiden name was Applewaite—but different fathers. Marvin never knew who his biological father was and Frankie's father never really accepted him but he was just part of the package when Joel Jessick married Frankie's mom. This is what I heard from Geordie after Marvin's suicide."

"Suicide?!?"

"Okay, this is what Geordie told me. He wasn't close to Marvin who was almost seven years older than him but Frankie was. There was only three years between them. Geordie described Marvin as always serious and a loner and with kind of a sour personality. Frankie and Geordie and their dad liked to kid around and play soccer and throw back a few beers but Marvin never joined in. He studied a lot and was a good student and he just sort of kept to himself. Then he went off to nursing school in Bridgetown...the real deal, Cave Hill! He won scholarships and everything so his step-dad never had to pay a cent and I doubt if he would have, anyway. His mother, Janie, always worked and apparently she helped him out with extra money for expenses as much as she could and Marvin worked while he was at school even though the curriculum was very demanding.

When Marvin was in his third year, he met this girl, Annette, and fell head over heels in love with her. He even bought her a ring and asked her to marry him when he was through with his courses. She took the ring and they were seeing each other pretty heavily for several months. Marvin was like a changed person, according to Geordie. He seemed really happy for the first time and more relaxed and he even slacked off on his studies a bit. But then, Annette met this older guy. He was really old—about twice her age, probably about 45. First, she was seeing him on the sly but then she finally told Marvin after this guy proposed to her. She said she was going to marry him and go to Canada—to Edmonton. She told him she could not take the chance on marrying Marvin and hanging around Barbados for the rest of her life. The world was way bigger than that and she wanted a piece of it. I got all this third hand because the only person Marvin confided in was Frankie, and after Marvin died, Frankie told Geordie.

Apparently, Marvin begged her not to do it, not to throw away their love for some old guy. But Annette replied that she was not really that into Marvin anyway and this old guy had more to offer her. Well, the day after graduation, she eloped with this guy and after that they left immediately for Canada and she's never been back since. Two days later, Marvin hung himself. He didn't even leave a note. Frankie just went crazy for a while according to Geordie."

"What do you mean? What happened?"

"Well, it was June then and he was taking this accelerated Licensed Practical Nurse course that took eleven months. It was finishing the end of that September and he was doing okay but he said he was going to drop out. According to Geordie, his mom was begging and pleading with him to hang in there and it took a couple of weeks before he agreed. Meanwhile, he'd missed a lot of classes and you can't do that in a course like that so she even paid for extra tutoring from a nurse instructor she knew to help him catch up. He told her he wanted to get away from Barbados for a couple of years and go to Canada but she didn't make the connection with Annette. The tutor helped him research the Foreign Workers program online and complete his application and Janie paid the application fee. Then he saw the position in Edmonton and applied for it. He didn't know Annette was working at Clive. He only knew she was in Edmonton. After that, he settled down and finished his program and you know the rest."

"He must have really loved his brother!" Claire said sadly.

"Yeah, I guess, but I think there was more to it than that. He really felt guilty for all those years when his father treated him so much better than Marvin and he knew how much Marvin felt it at times but didn't try to do anything to make it stop. He felt that he should have exerted some influence over his father to get him to behave better towards Marvin."

"Yes, I can see why he would feel that way," Tia said thoughtfully.

Chapter 41—They Actually Have Some Fun

At that point, Rosalina called the three of them for lunch. Aurora had been in the kitchen helping her. They sat down to a huge meal with many items Claire and Tia had never tasted before including *cou cou*, a dish made of cornmeal and okra, and fried flying fish to start, and a summer pudding made with various berries and Barbadian cherries pressed in a bread mold to finish. Afterword, they just sat around relaxing with full stomachs and Tia and Claire asked them to discuss the various island hotspots.

"Harrison's Cave sounds very interesting. We would love to see it. Can we repay your wonderful hospitality by treating you to a day trip there?"

"The beginning of a frown crossed Tia's face, not because she disapproved of the idea but because, as usual, Claire had barged ahead impetuously without consulting her first. However, she quickly suppressed it and warmly echoed her agreement.

"Benson and I need to work, and anyway we have already been there many times—but why don't you two go?" she asked, turning to her children.

"I don't know," Jeremy said. "I do have some commitments this week. What day did you have in mind?"

Claire automatically opened her mouth to respond but Tia decided it was time she took the initiative. "It really doesn't matter to us. Our only other big plan is to visit the Bridgetown market to buy gifts to take home and maybe a memento or two. So unless there is a special market day, it's entirely up to you. But remember, we leave on Sunday."

"Well you better visit the market on Saturday, then," Aurora said. "That would be the best day to listen to the steel drums, sample some authentic Bajan delicacies including various rums, see all the handicrafts and the stilt walkers and maybe take in some sponge music. And any other day is fine for me to go to the Cave. I'm between jobs right now," she added, with a grin.

"Great! How about Thursday, then? Would that work for you, too, Jeremy?" Claire asked, seizing back the initiative.

"Yeah, man!" he replied with a naughty grin. Jeremy was not one to let work or study commitments get in the way of a great opportunity to enjoy himself for free! His mother looked at them both with a slight frown but just shook her head and let it pass. She knew that in the end, Jeremy would do what he had to do to finish his education and get a decent job. And one day soon Aurora would get bored with just hanging around the house and start seriously looking for work.

"Thursday it is then!" Claire agreed. "By the way, what is sponge music?"

"It's a combination of calypso and ska and it started right here in Barbados in the '60's!" Aurora replied.

Claire still looked quizzical and Aurora added, "You will know it when you hear it at the market. It has a really unique backbeat!" Claire got a calculating smile on her face and Tia knew exactly what she was thinking. Jessie loved hearing different kinds of music, particularly when the music had a strong beat!

Jeremy drove Claire and Tia back to their hotel later that afternoon. They rested in their room for a while before showering and changing for dinner. They congratulated themselves on how they had been able to combine duty with fun and meet some great new people in the process!

The next day was Tuesday and they spent much of that day and the following one trying to figure out how to substantiate Jeremy's third hand story about Frank. They wanted to see the school where Frank and Annette had completed their nursing degrees but realized there would be no students there now who would know them and no way to access school records. They settled instead on a trip to the newspaper morgue of Barbados' main daily paper, *The Nationnews*. Supplied with Marvin's last name and the approximate date of his suicide they were able to access back copies describing the incident and even found a human interest story contributed by one reporter who discussed Marvin's history, his dreams for the future and his devastation over the loss of the woman he loved. Unfortunately, Annette's name was not mentioned, probably for liability reasons, but they did find her marriage announcement after much tedious digging even though they did not know her maiden name, because Crombie had only let them know her husband's name. Tia had the idea to check the newspaper for a list of graduates from their nursing college that year and fortunately the paper had printed one and they were able to match Annette's maiden name printed there to the wedding announcement. Claire noted sadly that Marvin had not won the Silver Medal that, according to Geordie he had long coveted for best overall standing during his four year nursing program. He must have been in no fit emotional state at the time to write his final exams. But at least he had graduated, likely because of his exceptionally strong standing throughout most of those four years. Armed with copies of these four different items of information, they hoped that Inspector McCoy would be convinced to follow up and they celebrated on

Wednesday evening with coconut chicken and prawn curry at a deceptively modest looking restaurant called Caribas.

Thursday morning, they met up with Aurora and Jeremy at the hotel and took the day long bus tour for Harrison's Cave from there. The experience was everything they could have hoped for. They saw a good stretch of the country on the way and the cave itself was like an elegant, underground city with the stalactites forming an endless dazzling array of ornate crystal chandeliers. At one point late in the day, Jeremy thought he saw Geordie back in the shadows of the cave. "If that is him would you like to meet him?" he asked Claire and Tia. "That way you could ask him directly about Frank."

Both of them felt an immediate frisson of fear and Tia replied, "No! He mustn't know who we are or what our connection to Frank is! It would be very bad if it got back to him. If you run into him later please be careful not to mention us!"

"O-o-o-kay," Jeremy drawled in a tone that suggested he thought they were being a bit paranoid about the issue and worrying for nothing. After that, Claire and Tia could no longer concentrate as fully on the amazing sights as they had done previously. At one point, there was a flash and Tia could not help wondering if the camera had been aimed at them.

Back at their hotel, they said good-bye to Jeremy and Aurora for the last time and Tia offered a final caution to Jeremy to be careful not to mention them when he saw Geordie again.

Friday, they took a belated bus tour of Bridgetown, and followed it in the afternoon with a two hour submarine excursion. At first, Tia demurred, put off by the $96.00 American price tag for the latter. But Claire pressed hard for the submarine tour, always one to get her licks in. When they returned from the tour, Tia had to agree it had been well worth it. They had descended to depths of 115 to 150 feet (35-45 meters) and viewed close up a rich variety of coral and tropical fish and even a couple of shipwrecks!

Saturday was a busy day at the market and Rosalina and Benson surprised them by joining them. Claire was thrilled by the spounge music and bought several cds for Jessie. Tia found a hand blown black glass Jaguar for Mavis. It was strung on a sturdy, tightly wound nylon cord that she calculated would not absorb drool readily. After sampling a variety of the island rums, they bought generous bottles for their men and one for Tia's father. For Tia's mother, she bought a delicate bracelet with a colorful glass-blown parrot dangling daintily from it. Mario's gift took more thought but then, in a book and magazine kiosk, she found a cardboard replica of Harrison's Cave paired with a colorful book detailing its history and geographic specifications. She knew that would be Mario's kind of thing!

The trip home on Sunday was long and tedious, involving two plane changes. In a rebellious effort to prolong the island spirit, they ordered Pina Coladas half way through the afternoon but had to settle for gin and tonics. Their loved ones awaited them at the airport, happy to have them back safe and sound and once they got there, they were happy to be home, too.

Chapter 42—Strange Things are Happening

On Monday morning, Tia received a phone call from the head of housekeeping at the Clive Centre begging her to come back to work for a few days. The person hired to take her place had been dismissed because of some inappropriate patient contact and another cleaner was off with the flu. They were really stuck. Although very tired from her long trip the day before, Tia agreed. She'd not been very happy about deserting them completely and this felt right to her.

As a result of this unexpected work commitment, Tia and Claire did not have a chance to confer until that evening as to their next step. After some discussion, they decided the best thing to do was to ask to see Inspector McCoy and Sergeant Crombie together, explaining that they'd uncovered new information pertinent to the case. They would tell them that the information was being handed over to Bill's lawyer as well, and that it would be introduced at Bill's Preliminary Hearing set for Thursday of that week. Tia and Claire had concluded that attempting to involve McCoy's supervisor, even if that were possible, would only inflame him and make him less likely to cooperate, even under duress.

Claire phoned McCoy's office as soon as Jessie left for school the next morning, at twenty to nine. She explained to the receptionist that she must talk to him urgently and to ask him to call her as soon as he came in. At 9:10, the phone rang.

"McCoy here. What can I do for you, Mrs. Marchysyn?"

Claire gritted her teeth but said nothing. He knew that she went by her maiden name but was busy patronizing her as usual. After a deliberate pause, she said, "I'm actually calling because there's something I can do for *you*. What time would you be able to see Ms. Ambrose and me this morning?"

"Just tell me now. There's no need to make a big ceremony out of it. I have things to do."

"Never mind, then," Claire retorted. "I'll just share it with Bill's lawyer so he'll be prepared to present it at the preliminary hearing on Thursday."

"I can spare you a few minutes at ten," McCoy replied, and hung up the phone.

Chapter 43—A Different Line of Investigation Begins

McCoy's office was just as they remembered it—bleak and officious looking. He greeted them with his perennial sneer, Sergeant Crombie at his side, and asked them to get down to business at once. They sat down and handed both officers separate copies of the newspaper articles they had unearthed.

"What's this?" McCoy asked coldly, after a cursory glance revealed nothing to his eyes of immediate interest.

"Frank Jessick's older brother, Marvin, committed suicide after his fiancée, Annette Richards, married an older Canadian man and went with him to Edmonton three years ago," Claire responded.

McCoy snatched the papers up and quickly glanced through them again. His shoulders relaxed and he crowed triumphantly, "It says here his last name is Applewaite. You've made a mistake!"

"Half-brother, three years apart, reported to be very close," Claire responded tersely and implacably.

"Reported by whom? How do *you* know?"

Claire did not answer his questions immediately. Instead she said, "After Marvin's death, Frankie told his younger brother, Geordie, that he was going to complete his Licensed Practical Nurse course, apply for foreign worker status in Canada and get a position in Edmonton. Then he was going to hunt Annette up and kill her for what she did to his brother. It was just uncanny luck that he ended up in the same institution as her."

"And you know this how?"

"His brother told a friend. His friend told us."

"And this *friend* who gave you this third hand information just happens to be in Edmonton?" McCoy asked sneeringly.

"No, he's in Barbados and..."

"*What?*" McCoy rose up in his chair in his agitation. "You went to *Barbados? Didn't I tell you not to interfere with this investigation?*"

Tia interjected at this point. "I work with someone from Barbados. It's a place I've always wanted to go. Claire and I needed a holiday and I suggested we go there. My friend asked me to look up her family and by sheer accident her younger brother happens to know Geordie." As an afterthought she added, "Barbados is a small place."

McCoy gave her a calculating look. "May I ask where you work?"

This of course was the very question Tia did not want him to ask but she could hardly refuse to answer. "At the Clive Centre," she said meekly.

"Oh," he replied in a deceptively calm voice. "And may I ask if you began working there before or after Annette Richards died?"

"I believe it was shortly after," Tia replied vaguely, and glanced helplessly at Claire.

McCoy turned venomously toward Claire. "I know this is your doing," he snarled. "You have deliberately interfered in a police investigation and contaminated the evidence after being specifically warned not to—and dragged this poor woman into it with you. I'm quite certain that this time I have enough evidence to bring charges."

"Excuse me," Tia said with an ominous coldness in her voice. Although Claire had good reason to be concerned at this point, she could not keep a little smirk off her face for she knew what was coming next. McCoy had hit a nerve with Tia.

"I am not a poor woman! I am not a poor dumb Italian! I have a mind of my own and I do what *I* think best. Here!" She thrust a wad of papers at him. "You will find a list of references who will tell you that I have been doing cleaning work for some time now and that their houses have never been cleaner than since they met and employed me. I have to find work that fits around my son's school schedule. I am not one of your clever Canadian women who farm their children out to others to bring up so they can fulfill themselves! But the trouble with piece work is it does not pay the bills so I was looking for a job that fit within my available weekday hours from 9:30 to 3. Here are two weeks of ads prior to the appearance of the ad from the Clive Centre. You tell me if you can find another cleaning job that fits within those hours and provides as many weekday hours of employment as that? I should mention that I have a number of long-term clients I did not feel I could abandon so I was not looking for a full-time position. Even cleaning ladies can have a sense of loyalty! Oh, and by the way, if you would like to question my employment at the Clive Centre any further you can check with the head of housekeeping there, Beulah Twain. You will find that I have had two promotions since I arrived and now oversee the cleaning staff on four different units on two floors. You will be told that I have improved the cleaning standards and improved work efficiency in the short while I have been there. All that work would not have left me much time for snooping as you are obviously suggesting!"

Claire stood up at this point. "So, in summary, we went to Barbados because we needed a holiday and were interested in seeing Barbados. Tia got the job at the Clive Centre because she needed a job and it was the only one that suited her hours during the period in which she was looking. And if in the process we have inadvertently uncovered evidence that may help a poor helpless man who cannot even speak for himself so be it. If you have any more concerns, please contact my lawyer, who is also Bill's lawyer by the way, and who will have plenty to say at the hearing on Thursday." Claire gave a meaningful glance at Tia and flounced towards the door. Tia followed.

Chapter 44—Grand Plans and Battle Plans

When they hit the street, Claire said, "Let's find a coffee shop. I need two double espressos and about five donuts." Tia said nothing but made sure to be in front of Claire when they found a Tim Horton's so she could place the order. "Two large coffees, half de-caf and half regular, and two plain cake donuts, please," she requested, when they reached the front of the line.

When they found a place to sit, Claire said peevishly, "You're being kind of officious, aren't you?"

"It's for your own good. You're already revved up and we need to be able to think. We may have won that battle but it doesn't mean we'll win the war."

They talked for a while about what McCoy might do and what they needed to do next on their respective long to-do lists but mostly they spent a quiet hour decompressing from the stressful interview they'd just had. While they'd been in Barbados, considerable progress had been made on readying the new house for occupancy. Jimmy, Fuji, his brother, Daisuke, and even Dan and Tia's father, when free of childcare responsibilities, had worked together to repaint the house, replace the Arborite on the kitchen counter and the worn-out kitchen sink and tap, and build a wheelchair ramp.

Most of the adaptations made to the house to date were for accommodating Mavis' extraordinary needs. Tia had purchased a surplus, second-hand hospital bed with movable side rails from the Clive Centre and it had been installed in Mavis' room.

The original bathtub in Mavis' bathroom had been replaced by a jet tub mounted on a 32-inch base constructed by Fuji and his brother. This would make bathing Mavis much easier for staff and Mavis would enjoy the jets. The old, discarded kitchen cabinet base had been laboriously carted up from the basement, repainted and a padded vinyl cover stapled to the top of it to serve as a change and dressing table for Mavis. The front door and her bedroom and bathroom doors had been widened and the doors replaced in order to accommodate her wheelchair. But for this, Jimmy had hired professional help. Although Fuji and his brother, Daisuke, had assured him they could do it, he felt that too many things could go wrong and also that it was just too much work to get through in the short time available.

Since Mavis had had her new power wheelchair for less than 90 days, Jimmy was able to return it, explaining that it was too bulky to be accommodated in her new living arrangements and that she had never been able to learn to manoeuver it on her own. This gave him some much needed financial flexibility to cover the cost of her renovations. They were still planning some basement remodeling, e.g., putting a shower in the downstairs bathroom and installing a wall furnace, again with professional help, to turn the downstairs recreation room into a comfortable den, but basically the upstairs was ready and quite habitable at this point. Tia devoted the remainder of the day to cleaning the new home since her parents had stayed on to help until the three roommates could move in. Claire met with the lawyer to update him on the new information and discuss strategy for Thursday's hearing.

Chapter 45—Bill's Day in Court

For a preliminary hearing, the courtroom was quite crowded with witnesses. Bill's lawyer, Jack Anders, had issued subpoenas for Frankie Jessick; Jennie Marlowe, the LPN who'd been on duty that night; Alma Theron, Bill's primary care nurse at Wild Rose Hospital; Bess Enright, the psychologist who'd assessed him; and somebody named Anna Loews. He was also planning to call Claire and Marion to the stand.

The crown attorney had subpoenaed Ivy Watson, the unit manager at the Clive Centre; as well as Judy Odin, the charge nurse who'd been on duty in Bill's unit on the day of the murder. And, of course, the coroner, Inspector McCoy and Sergeant Crombie. Bill was at the hospital where a video conferencing system was in place to gather testimony from him if necessary and two policemen were also in attendance there, in case the stress of the situation caused him to act out.

When the crown attorney, James Albright, had Inspector McCoy on the stand, he asked him about opportunity to commit the crime. McCoy declared that Bill had had ample opportunity, and this gave Jack Anders the opening on cross-examination to ask if anyone else could have had that opportunity. Once Frank's name was mentioned, he was able to pursue the question of means and to that end called Anna Loews to the stand. She stated her name and occupation. She worked in the kitchen at the Clive Centre and had been on supper duty the evening before Annette Richards was killed.

"Can you identify this knife?" Jack Anders asked her, showing her a knife in a plastic bag with some blood still in evidence on the blade.

"It looks like the knife I used to use to cut the sandwiches for the evening snack."

"Did you use this knife that evening before Annette Richards' murder to cut the sandwiches?"

"No, when I looked for it at 7:30, the time when I usually start cutting the sandwiches, I could not find it anywhere. I had to use a shorter knife which did not do as clean a job. I remember the kitchen supervisor raised her eyebrows when she saw the sandwiches."

"When was the last time you saw it before that?"

"I think I saw it in its usual place when I came on duty at four that afternoon but I can't swear to that."

"And where was its usual place?"

"It used to hang on a rack just inside the door between the kitchen and the patient dining room."

"Did you see anybody come into the kitchen who was not doing kitchen work that night?"

"Yes, Frankie Jessick came in about 5:30." This admission resulted in a low murmur echoing through the courtroom and the judge demanded order.

"Do you know what he was doing there?"

"Yes, one of his patients had fallen during an epileptic seizure and smashed his front teeth. He was on a pureed diet and Frank came in to get his special meal as he was responsible for feeding him."

"Did you see the knife in the kitchen after that?"

"No, but like I said, I never looked for it until I needed it to cut the sandwiches later."

The prosecuting lawyer asked two additional questions of Anna on cross-examination before she was allowed to leave the stand. "Did you see anybody else who did not regularly work in the kitchen enter it that night?"

"No."

"Did you leave the kitchen at any time that evening?"

"Oh, yes. I was back and forth between the kitchen and the dining room a lot because I had to help feed some of the clients but it directly connects to the kitchen and I would have seen if anybody went in there who didn't belong."

"Did you leave the area at all that evening?"

"Yes, I took my own supper break between 6:15 and 6:45, just before I had to make the sandwiches. I went downstairs to the staff lunchroom."

"So anyone else could have gone into the kitchen at that time and you would not have known."

"I suppose so," she said doubtfully.

"Please explain what you mean. Could they or could they not have entered the kitchen during that time?"

"Well, technically not. We are supposed to maintain very strict hygiene standards. No unauthorized personnel are supposed to be allowed in the kitchen, not even nurses. And *certainly* not patients! I would have *heard* about *that*, even a couple of days later if not that evening. I had the next day off."

"Thank you, Ms. Loews. No further questions."

Because of the long list of witnesses, the hearing took the whole day. After lunch, Jack introduced the video conferencing with Bill which gave the presiding judge his first opportunity to see the supposed main suspect in the murder. Bill was looking very meek and withdrawn and when asked if he remembered the murder and the evening before the murder, he could not respond coherently. When asked if he remembered Annette with a picture of her displayed on his video screen, Bill withdrew involuntarily. "She *mean!* I don't *like* her," he responded.

"She's dead, Bill. She was murdered."

"I don't care. I don't *like* her." At that point, Bill stopped talking and started rocking and the interview had to be discontinued.

Throughout the course of the afternoon, Jack Anders called several witnesses to the stand. One was Jennie Marlowe, the Licensed Practical Nurse on the unit where Bill had been at the Clive Centre.

"Can you tell me if Bill received any medication on the evening in question?"

"Yes, he did."

"Can you please tell the court what that medication was, what its effects are and when it was administered and in what dosage."

"He was given 5 mg. of haloperidol, an antipsychotic drug also used to curb aggression and tics, at nine that evening. I administered it myself orally."

"Was he taking that medication routinely?"

"No. It was administered as a prn."

"Why was it given to him that night?"

"To curb any further aggression. He had struck out against the nurse who was killed that morning when she tried to convince him to remain in his chair at breakfast. And during the supper hour, he was roaming around the dining room. We did not try to stop him because of the morning incident. We were afraid he would lash out again."

"How does the drug act and what are its side effects?"

"I don't know. I just followed the doctor's orders and gave it to him."

"What time did he go to sleep that night?"

"By ten o'clock he appeared to be asleep."

"What do you mean, "*appeared* to be asleep?"

"Well for all I know he could have cheeked the drug and pretended to be asleep. It would not be the first time a patient has tried that."

"I see. Was there any evidence of that? For example, did you find a discarded pill or discoloration on the sheet from it?"

"N-o-o," Jennie replied somewhat grudgingly.

In what position was he lying?"

"He was on his back."

Jennie was dismissed from the stand at this point and the Clive Center pharmacist, Manny Oswald, was called up. After the usual preliminaries and after ascertaining that he had familiarized himself with the Clive charting records on Bill, he was asked about the effects of haloperidol.

"Haloperidol blocks the uptake of serotonin and dopamine and its general effect therefore is to mellow people out. In persons not used to taking it on a regular basis, it also has a powerful sedating effect."

"What is the likelihood that Bill would have awakened later in the night after receiving .5 mg. of haloperidol at 9 p.m.?"

"I would say it would be low but not impossible. Occasionally, an individual will have a paradoxical reaction from haloperidol and become hyperactive rather than somnolent."

"If Bill did awaken during the night in question would he have been capable of slipping into the hall unnoticed, quietly approaching the deceased from behind so she did not hear him and stabbing her in the back?" Jack Anders asked.

"It is likely that both gross and fine motor control would have still been compromised to some degree and that he would have made sufficient noise in the hall, either by stumbling slightly or by shuffling his feet, that he would have been heard by anyone awake and within hearing range."

Jack next called Claire to the stand and determined from her testimony that the pictures she had taken at the scene, which he placed in evidence, suggested that Bill had been framed since they indicated right hand use of the knife and it could be clearly established that he was strongly left handed.

Jack next called Inspector McCoy to the stand. He asked him why he'd determined Bill to be the principal suspect at the time of the incident.

"Well, the evidence was on him, wasn't it?—and nobody else appeared to have had the opportunity to kill Ms. Richards."

"Has any other possible suspect since been identified?"

"Yes, new evidence has recently come to light and a second possible suspect identified and we're following up on it."

"Does this new suspect have a motive as strong as or stronger than the motive that has been attributed to my client?"

"Yes," McCoy replied tersely.

"Please state this suspect's name and explain the circumstances that would make this person a credible suspect for Ms. Richards' murder."

McCoy explained Frankie Jessick's connection to the deceased. He stated that the police in Barbados had been advised and had interviewed Frankie's brother, Geordie. Under police interrogation, he'd broken down and admitted that Frankie had threatened to kill Annette to avenge his brother. The police had a signed affidavit to that effect and had faxed a copy to his office. As previously agreed, no mention was made of the role Claire and Tia had played in order to protect them, and the result was that McCoy looked better than he deserved to look under the circumstances. Claire gritted her teeth at this when she recalled how willfully obdurate McCoy had been in the face of contrary evidence, and what it had cost Bill.

Bess was called to the stand next. She testified both to Bill's lack of any aggressive outbursts in the past except for those rare instances of a defensive response. She also described how much he'd deteriorated in the past three weeks and how he currently presented as depressed and disoriented and even apparently losing some of his daily living skills. She stated that if he remained in the hospital much longer, she had no doubt that the deterioration in his functioning would become permanent. Angry rumbling followed these remarks and the judge had to again call for order in the court.

In his concluding arguments, Jack stated that there had been insufficient evidence to retain his client in the first place. He should have been released back into the community under the supervision of his guardians if the Clive supervisor had been unwilling for him to remain in that facility. And he certainly should not be in the hospital now when another suspect had been identified with better means, motive and opportunity to have murdered the deceased. He asked that his client be released immediately and without prejudice if at least one of his guardians were willing to undertake his supervision and Marion had already testified earlier that she would do so. Jimmy had not been able to be in court that day because of the intensive, last minute work on the house.

The crown attorney requested that Frank Jessick be commanded to remain in Edmonton and available for further questioning and that he relinquish his passport since he was a flight risk. He'd been requested to bring it with him to court. James Albright did not object to

Jack's request that Bill be released into the community under the supervision of his aunt.

In issuing his verdict, the judge admonished Inspector McCoy for being responsible for the ordeal Bill had been put through on the basis of such questionable evidence. He released Bill unconditionally and without prejudice into the community under the supervision of his guardian as lacking sufficient means, motive and opportunity to have committed the murder in question. However, he did say that if new evidence emerged in the future suggestive of Bill's involvement he could be re-arrested and re-tried. He also agreed to the restrictions on Frank Jessick's departure.

Chapter 46—Bill Moves Again—Hopefully for the Last Time

It was four o'clock in the afternoon by the time court was dismissed. It had been a long day already but Bess, Marion, Claire, Gus and Amanda met up at Amanda's house to discuss the next steps and Tia joined them there soon after. Tia had stopped at home first when she returned from work so she could bring over her latest cake creation, coconut-oatmeal. They all sat around the kitchen table eating the surprisingly rich and flavorful cake, drinking coffee and gleefully reviewing the judge's censure of McCoy, and Bill's release from suspicion. Then they moved with their coffee cups to the more comfortable living room chairs and hashed over Frankie's defiant refusal to admit that he had done the murder.

"Some people just can never take responsibility for their wrongs!" was Amanda's way of understanding Frankie's adamant denial.

"Well, I think our next step is to get Bill out of that hospital, tonight if possible," Marion said. "I've been just waiting on tenterhooks every day for him to have a major blow-out. I know the house isn't ready yet but I thought I'd ask Hilda if he can come and stay with me in her house until everything is organized."

"From what you've told me about her, it doesn't seem likely that she's going to like *that* idea very much," Claire responded.

"She doesn't have to like it. She just has to put up with it and treat Bill decently—and she *will* because she knows the consequences otherwise in terms of me changing my will," Marion said grimly.

Although many there were quietly glad to hear Marion standing up for herself against her daughter, Bess had other ideas. "Marion, I agree with you that we need to get Bill out of the hospital as soon as possible. Tonight might not work though because you'll need Doctor Milton to sign him out. I can call and see if she's still there. She often works late. But, in any case, I don't agree with him moving temporarily to your daughter's house. For one thing, he'll pick up that he's not wanted. You can't fool him on something like that. And for another, having to get used to another house only to move again in a short time will be too disruptive for him and only set him back further. It would be better for him to stay where he is than to have to move twice."

Claire looked thoughtful and stole a glance at Tia. Tia thought for a moment and then nodded her head almost imperceptibly. She was quite sure she knew what her impetuous friend was going to suggest. Claire cleared her throat and began.

"I think we should just grab the bull by the horns (Tia smirked at this, thinking it was always one of Claire's favorite strategies) and just move Bill directly into the new house now. The work on the main floor is done and during the day Mavis and her assistant can come over for visits or Roscoe can come to see him—or you and Amanda could go over, Aunt Gus. Or if there is too much noise from the basement renovations going on, he could go over to see Mavis. Do you think that could be worked out with her caregiver, Tia? And Marion, you could just move into Mavis' room at the home there for the time being and stay with him at night—and if you need help, one of us could come over and spend the night. We could take turns...and then when we have the meeting with PDD this week they would see that the die is already cast (*Claire did love her clichés*, Tia thought) and they would be more likely to push for funding for the three of them right away!"

Claire finished this last comment in a rush and looked around the room to see how everyone was taking it. There was dead silence. Bess wondered if she should weigh in but then thought better of it. There was something going on in this room that was beyond her experience. She looked around and saw subtle changes in peoples' body language. Backs straightened, feet planted more firmly on the floor, eyes brightened. The air seemed charged. What she was seeing and feeling was the birth of an advocacy group, the sudden sense of power that people feel when they realize that if they work together they can make something happen that they all dearly want to happen.

Surprisingly—or not—Aunt Gus was the first to speak. In another life she would have made a good fifth columnist so the notion of sticking a spoke in the wheel of the system held a natural appeal for her. "Tia, is the main floor cleaned up from all the renovations?"

"I cleaned it thoroughly on Tuesday and I asked the guys to do whatever sawing is left for the downstairs renovations outside. There might still be a little dust floating around, though. No use getting the furnace cleaned until everything is finished. But I don't think Bill has any allergies, does he, Marion?" Marion shook her head.

"Well, I have an extra air purifier I won't be using until our own basement renovations are done. We can put that in there and it should help with the dust," Gus said, in a burst of generosity not characteristic for her. "I say we go get him right now. We can *do* this!"

"I've got to get back there in any case,' Marion said. "He's been alone too long. It would be awful if something happened now!"

Tia looked thoughtful. Then she heard the front door open. Jimmy came in.

"Hi," she said. "What are you doing here? Who's with Mavis?"

"Nice to see you, too!" he said, and leaned over her chair and kissed her proprietorially.

"I asked the caregiver to stay an extra hour because I knew you people were over here plotting," Jimmy said with a laugh. Marion had phoned him at work to let him know what had happened in court so they did not need to review that with him. He sat down with a piece of cake and cup of coffee and was updated by the others on the latest plans.

"Jimmy, would *you* take Marion to the hospital and pick up Bill and his things, please? He knows you and is less likely to be upset that way," Tia asked.

"Sure. I can do that. We can leave any time. We should probably let him have his supper there first, though. You know he likes to eat at the same time every day."

"Well, I'll be moving into the house with him, so I need you to stop at Hilda's house on the way so I can pack a bag to get me by for a few days. By the time that's done and we get to the hospital, his supper time will be over."

"Okay, let's go!"

"Yeah, let's *do* this!" Gus said, obviously still pumped.

Claire looked at her in amusement and then rose from her chair. "I have to leave, too." Dan's away and Amy's home alone with Jessie. I have to make sure she gets a decent supper because that certainly isn't something Amy can do!"

"I thought you had all Jessie's supper meals prepared in advance?" Tia queried.

"I do but she never makes sure that Jessie drinks enough and she often does not puree her fruit for dessert fine enough and then Jessie chokes."

"I thought you were going to get rid of her?"

"I was looking for a new person when I found you that position at Clive Centre and then I got sidetracked with all that's been happening since." Jimmy glowered at this but did not say anything. Marion was already up and standing at the door and the three of them left together.

Tia called after Jimmy, "I'm going to make up the beds for Bill and Marion and take some food over for breakfast. May I use an extra set of Mavis' sheets to make up Bill's bed until Marion can get organized?"

"Sure, take whatever you need. What's important is to keep Bill from getting upset while he's making this transition. Maybe we should bring Mavis over to see him when you arrive. The ramp is done. We just need to do the final staining and get the anti-skid strips on but the weather is dry so we should be able to make it up and down."

"Oh, thank you, Jimmy!" Marion said gratefully. "That's a good idea. It should make him happy and help to keep him calm." Marion was beginning to feel the weight of what she had committed to, living alone with Bill for the next while, and she was feeling a little nervous.

Hilda was home when they arrived at her house and Marion explained what had happened that day and what her immediate plans were. Predictably, Hilda objected, claiming that it would be too hard on Marion, and Bill ought to just stay where he was until everything was in place. But the old timid, stuttering Marion seemed to have disappeared and she turned on Hilda somewhat fiercely. "If you had been able to make time to visit him in these past two weeks you would know what kind of state he's in. It's getting worse every day and that's not just me saying it. The psychologist said it in court today. That situation is ending now, just as soon as I can get up there!" And with that, Marion went into her room, closed her door and started packing.

    Just as they had all feared, Bill was nervous about leaving the hospital, even though he clearly did not like it there. But any change was always very hard for him because of his autistic condition, and doubly so because of his limited cognitive capacity to process it. However, Jimmy talked to him in soothing tones and explained that Mae-Mae was waiting there to see him.
    Meanwhile, Marion quickly and quietly packed up Bill's possessions and asked an orderly to take them down to the door nearest to where the car was parked. Then she completed the check-out procedure at admission. Fortunately, Bess had been able to get through to Dr. Milton in time and she had signed Bill out before leaving for the day. Meanwhile, Jimmy was taking Bill around the ward to say good-by to everyone and then he gently and leisurely brought him downstairs to join Marion. She stayed with Bill while Jimmy loaded the luggage and then they drove off. But Jimmy stopped a short distance away and asked Bill to wave good-bye to the hospital so he would understand that he was finally leaving it. Bill said nothing all the way home but seemed calm and happy.
    Jimmy had phoned ahead and Mavis was waiting for them at the new house when they got there. The table was set for supper since only Bill and Mavis had eaten at this point. Bill pulled a chair close to Mavis' wheelchair, sat down next to her and took hold of her

hand. He started the happy chanting he liked to do and which nobody had heard from him in weeks. "Mae-Mae, Mae-Mae, good day, my day, my Mae, Mae-Mae, Mae-Mae." Bill rocked gently back and forth with a peaceful smile on his face as he chanted.

Marion looked at Bill and Mavis with tears of happiness in her eyes. "He's going to be alright, isn't he," she said, turning towards the others, more statement than question. Jimmy and Tia could only nod their heads because they both had big lumps in their throats.

Chapter 47—PDD Agrees

The next day, the day of the fateful PDD meeting, was cool and drizzly. Claire and Tia together had strategized that it would be best to hold the meeting in Jimmy's house, but to move Mavis and her assistant over to the new house for the period of the meeting. Gus and Amanda would accompany them and play Canasta with the assistant. Marion thought she'd better stay with Bill, and Jimmy would be representing her at the meeting as Bill's co-guardian as well as Mavis' guardian. Roscoe and his uncle would be visiting with Bill and Mavis at the new house while his parents, Fuji and Yuna, attended the meeting. Of course, the PDD personnel would be visiting the people at the house and also looking the house over but this way they would not be spending enough time to notice too many of the flaws that still remained despite all the frantic work that had been done over the last two weeks since they had gained possession. Also, the families would be able to conduct the meeting in a peaceful, tastefully furnished environment with no distractions and few enough people to encourage open communication. Claire had worked it all out in this calculated way and Tia could not help thinking that there was a little of Aunt Gus' conniving ways in her! Tia's big concern, on the other hand, was that nobody track dirt from the sleet-wet street into either house and that there was not enough space for all those people to park their shoes in a reasonable order at the front door of either house. She was also simultaneously baking cakes in the ovens of both houses because she wanted them to smell homey and welcoming so she was busy running back and forth to check on them and that all the necessary fixings for coffee and cake were on both kitchen tables. The cake for the new house was chocolate-potato which should be nice and dense and moist and the cake for Jimmy's house was sour cream spice cake. She fretted that she could not do icings since they were being cooked at the last moment to enhance the aroma and would be too warm to frost. However, Claire assured her it would be less messy this way and nobody would mind.

The PDD team arrived promptly at two in two separate cars. Claire had asked them to come first of all to the new house so they could meet Mavis, Bill and Roscoe as well as the others including Marion. There were three of them, Anita, the PDD intake worker; Ben, one of the coordinators for agency-run homes; and Irene, one of the original family-managed program staff. Claire had requested representatives from both areas and was relieved to see that they had been able to accommodate her. After introductions, Anita asked what the status was for Bill in terms of the murder charge. Claire said, "Well, maybe you would like to hear from the judge himself," and she turned on a small tape recorder that accommodated mini-tapes and played his closing remarks, dismissing Bill without prejudice and censuring Inspector McCoy for his mistreatment of him.

Marion gasped and blurted out, "Claire, didn't you see all the signs about no recording devices allowed?"

Claire just shrugged her shoulders and said, "I only taped the part about Bill. You can't expect these people to just take our word for it that he was fully cleared."

Ben interjected then. "Well, he wasn't exactly fully cleared. More like cleared for the time being. Somebody must have killed that nurse and until that somebody is identified, the possibility will always remain open that it could have been him, unlikely maybe but not impossible."

"Well, they're investigating another suspect who's emerged and the case against him is way stronger than the superficial evidence they had against Bill—but I couldn't exactly record that part of the proceedings. It wouldn't have been right!"

Aunt Gus snorted, wordlessly pointing out that none of the recording had been right! Meanwhile, Bill had taken Mavis' hand and was chanting, "Mae-Mae, Mae-Mae, my Mae, my Mae."

Where had he picked up the possessive pronoun? And why now of all times? Marion wondered nervously, as she noted Irene frowning in Bill's direction. People with autism rarely used pronouns—and never possessive pronouns.

Claire said smoothly, "It's amazing how Bill's mood has lifted in just the few hours he's been away from the hospital. I wish Bess, the hospital psychologist who assessed him, could see him now. She said she'd come to this meeting if she could get away from work on time. She's planning to sit on the board we are establishing, you know." As if on cue, Bess magically arrived. Claire pointed silently to Bill and Mavis and waved her head just slightly towards Irene before even introducing Bess to the PDD staff. Meanwhile, Bill was obligingly continuing his chant and Bess understood the concerned looks she was seeing. "Well!" she said brightly. "Bill certainly seems happier now!" But I guess we'll save that discussion for the meeting. I only have an hour, Claire, so I hope we'll be starting soon."

"In just a few minutes, Bess. We're going over to Jimmy's house for the meeting but I promised these people a quick tour of the house, first." To herself,

Claire was thinking triumphantly, *Ha! This gives me a good reason for keeping the house inspection brief!*

Claire first showed them the set-up in Mavis' room, pointing out the raised bath tub, and mentioning how much easier that would make bathing Mavis for the staff. She explained how they'd been able to come by the bed and commented that when Mavis moved in, bed cushions would be provided to keep her positioned correctly and to protect her feet from hitting the rails if she had a seizure. Claire then pointed out the ceiling tracks and mentioned that they'd already been able to access a ceiling lift so staff would not be expected to lift. She pointed out the large change counter with built-in cupboards underneath to accommodate all of Mavis's special equipment and supplies and commented that staff would be using the toilet and sink in Mavis' bathroom since Mavis now used a commode, having recently been retrained. Claire took pains to stress that the other clients in the home would not have access to Mavis's room. Tia glanced quickly at their faces and saw that they were quite impressed with the arrangements that had been made for Mavis so far.

Claire led the staff briskly through the rest of the house, pointing out the shower facilities in the main bathroom and stressing that Bill and Roscoe were routinely in the habit of taking showers and never baths. She spent little time in the kitchen which was neat and attractive with its new paint job, sink and counter. She pointed out the furniture arrangements throughout with plenty of room for Mavis to cruise around in her chair and ample space for her at the dining room table. Then, knowing that at least the women were probably feeling some nervousness about all three of the young people sleeping in such close quarters on the main floor, she led them downstairs and explained the plans for developing bedrooms there for Bill and Roscoe, pointing out the large windows for fire escape and the recreation room where they could play games or watch TV without disturbing Mavis. Lastly, she took them to the planned new bathroom with the plumbing already "roughed in" and explained that this would likely be where Bill and Roscoe would take most of their showers and that they would not be accessing the main bathroom upstairs if they got up at night. She then led them back upstairs and pointed out the small bedroom directly next to the master bedroom where Mavis would be sleeping. "I was thinking this could be the staff bedroom," she said, "and maybe we could put an adjoining door right here that could stay open at night so staff could easily hear and see Mavis if she woke up and had any problems. That way we could probably get by with sleep night staff which would be cheaper. What do you think?"

Tia, always the observant one, noticed the positive effect this statement had on the PDD staff, since it addressed two of their likely concerns in one stroke—Mavis' safety and finances for this high needs home. She noticed the quirk of Bess' mouth and gathered that she was also appreciating Claire's strategy.

After this brief tour, the PDD personnel said their good-byes to Bill, Roscoe, Mavis, Marion and Daisuke, Roscoe's uncle, and the rest of them adjourned to Jimmy's house to commence the meeting. Anita, the intake worker, explained that funding approval had come through for Mavis and Bill and would likely be in place for Roscoe the following week. They had not been able to attain full 24/7 funding but Claire's suggestion that they could manage with overnight sleep staff instead of awake staff made the situation considerably easier, so it was likely that under those circumstances the families would only have to arrange to cover one afternoon shift a week themselves. PDD personnel would be setting up some training sessions for the guardians for the coming week to orient them to the administrative details involved and the requirements in terms of staff qualifications. After the first two sessions, they could begin interviewing and hiring staff. Until all of that training was fully in place and PDD was satisfied that they were operating according to the rules, they would not be permitted to leave staff alone with the clients unsupervised so that meant that one of them would have to be in the house at all times, likely for the next couple of weeks.

Claire interjected at this point to ask if any other of the informal Board members could take shifts for the next two weeks to spell the guardians off. Bess quickly volunteered, stating that she had some holiday time coming up and wanted to spend time at the home so she could help out with suggestions for activities and schedules. It was quite obvious that this suggestion met with their approval and even relief that a trained professional would be so closely involved.

"I can probably cover some shifts as well," Aunt Gus said with a slightly discernible self-importance. I know them all better than Bess, you see."

After a slight pause, Anita said rather weakly, "Uh, thank you. That would be helpful."

"Me, too," Amanda chimed in.

"I'm sure my brother would take some shifts," Fuji added.

"We will probably set up three training sessions for you for next week, right here in the home," Anita added. "That way we can also see how you are working things out and offer support and suggestions. One thing we need to hash out is day programming. There's also the question of male vs. female staff. You have two big guys here. If they ever get into it, you're going to need some muscle around to control the situation."

"Ah, but that's the beauty of our arrangement!" Amanda said proudly. Gus and I are right across the street and we're usually home. We can be over here in a couple of minutes if needed. And Claire's husband works at home and he's only a couple of minutes away by car. And Tia and Jimmy will also be around much of the time. And I also have neighbors on this street I'm hoping to get involved. I have lived here for 30 years, you know—and I know a lot of people!"

"Well once we provide you with PDD funding, the onus will be on *us* to oversee the situation and ensure you are following the prescribed guidelines so you can expect us to be closely involved at first," Ben said. "Also, anyone who wants to volunteer in the home will have to go through our training sessions before being considered eligible and have a satisfactory criminal record check. Both staff and volunteers should have CPR training but we can give you a little leeway on that since none of the clients are medically fragile. Anita and Irene both nodded their heads in agreement.

"That's fine with us," Claire said. "That's what we want. We know we have a lot to learn and it won't be easy."

Tia had waited until now to speak and she said, "I have resigned from my supervisory position at the Clive Centre and have agreed to go in only on a consultant basis as my schedule allows. I will be here every day for part of the time and covering when no one else is available."

"What did you do there?" Irene asked, innocently.

"I was in charge of housekeeping on two of their floors" Tia said, somewhat defensively. "They needed some help to raise their hygiene standards but I have things pretty well set in place there now." She braced herself to see the usual dismissal of such efforts but instead saw respect on the women's faces, especially

Irene's, and a neutral, non-judgmental look on Ben's face.

"That's great!" Irene responded. "People don't take cleaning seriously enough in hospitals. They think swabbing a mop from room to room is cleaning. No wonder there are so many infections!"

"Exactly," Tia said, enthusiastically. "And…." But Claire cut her off at this point. She had noticed Bess shuffling around preparatory to leaving.

"I think Bess is leaving and it's getting late. We probably all need to get going," she said.

The meeting broke up and Anita told them that she would be in touch in the morning to set up the PDD appointments. She left a packet of papers with Tia and asked her to go through them and follow the guidelines for hiring staff. Then they left just a couple of minutes after Bess. Fuji and Yuna went back across the street, saying they had to collect his brother and son as Randy's wife would be expecting them back there for dinner. Gus and Amanda went home to check on the cats.

Chapter 48—Time to Relax; Time to Reflect

When the door closed behind the last of them, Claire went to the fridge, pulled out the bottle of Stoneleigh Sauvignon Blanc she'd stored there earlier, grabbed a couple of wine glasses and plopped herself down in Jimmy's favorite armchair in the living room. Tia sat down neatly in a nearby rocker. Claire poured the wine and handed Tia her glass. "We did it!" she crowed.

"Why do you Canadians think drinking is the only way to celebrate?" Tia asked quizzically.

"Come off it!" Claire groaned. "Spending your first two years in Italy does not qualify you as a permanent alien in Canada. And secondly, don't you think we deserve this after all we have been through? Don't you think we *need* to celebrate this moment?"

"Not if it means getting a ticket for drunk driving on the way home!"

"Here's to hard work and joylessness," Claire said sarcastically, raising her glass and then half draining it.

Jimmy walked in then, grinning. Clearly he'd overheard the last two exchanges. "Claire is right, you know, Tia. What we have all accomplished in such a short period of time is amazing and none of it would have happened without her. You *should* be celebrating, so you girls go ahead and drink your faces off. I'll drive you both home in about an hour. I just came over to pick up Mavis's meal and I have take-out for Bill and Marion and me. The evening assistant is there now with Mavis."

Jimmy left but his admonition had brought about a change in Tia. She allowed herself to feel for the first time all that they'd accomplished, and relaxed and sipped her wine. The next hour was spent reviewing the events of the day and making plans for the coming week.

"What are we going to do about a team leader?" Tia asked. "I suppose I can take on that role for the time being."

"No!" Claire said forcefully. "I have a better idea. What about Denise? She told you that she was interested in this kind of work—and that way you would know that the house would always be clean," she added, half humorously but with a serious glint in her eye.

"What? And leave the Clive Center without either of us?"

"You can go back there once everything is settled if you love it so much!"

"No, my responsibility is here now, making sure Mavis is okay."

"Don't say that," Claire begged. You don't know what it's like—to never be free—to always have to think in hours, not days. To never know what tomorrow holds. Don't take that on if you don't have to."

Tia looked closely at Claire and saw the tired lines under her eyes that she'd been too preoccupied to notice earlier. "How has Jessie been lately?" she asked.

"She's been up a lot at night—but don't change the subject. This is not about Jessie."

But it was, Tia thought to herself. "Okay," Tia said. "As it happens, I'm going into the Clive Centre tomorrow and I'll talk to Denise. She did a lot of talking to the rest of the staff while I was gone and some of them have come around pretty well. Things are going more smoothly there. The main center supervisor called me into her office the other day when I was there and asked me if I'd consider coming back and taking over the supervision of the housekeeping staff for the entire building. The head housekeeper is leaving at the end of the month. I've been thinking about it. I really don't want to be financially dependent on Jimmy and I do want my own career. I have some ideas I'd like to develop—and maybe I'd even like to write a book about them." This last Tia said somewhat defensively.

Claire looked at her friend affectionately. "That's what I want for you, for you to be yourself and not somebody's drudge—and I'm sure that's what Jimmy wants for you, too, even if it *is* his own sister we're talking about!"

Chapter 49—New Threat

Tia got her chance to talk to Denise at the Clive Centre the next day at their morning coffee break which they'd arranged to spend together. She was surprised at her response.

"Oh!" Denise gasped. "I've been so hoping that you would ask me!"

"But I thought you liked it here," Tia replied. "And you are so *good* at your job!"

"Thank you. I try my best. I like things to be properly cleaned but it's not my passion like it is yours. It's more like a means to an end. But in the final analysis it is just drudgery—and I'm tired of being somebody else's drudge."

"But what do you think it will be like to look after somebody who's completely helpless, to have to feed her and bathe her and change her and wash her clothes and administer her medication and do her range of motion exercises every day—and countless other things?"

"Is she happy when you do those things for her? Can she smile at you or let you know when she needs you for something? Walls don't do that for you no matter how many times you wash them."

Tia realized something at that moment. The old saying that, "One man's meat is another man's poison," apart from its sexist connotation, was really true. And, in any case, she did not love cleaning per se. She loved the theory behind cleaning. How to do a better job with less effort and how to create a pleasant, home-like environment that people wanted to be in. And with a sudden sobering chill, Tia also realized something else. She wanted to be like a sister to Mavis, to make sure that she was okay and that the people who looked after her did right by her—but she did not want to be her primary care provider. For her, that would represent drudgery way more than washing a floor or cleaning a toilet. But she could not tell Jimmy this. She hardly dared admit it to herself. Yet Claire had known. She smiled at the thought of Claire and her amazing perspicacity.

Chapter 50—Things Get Interesting

Tia and Denise arranged to get together that evening so Denise could meet Bill and Mavis and they parted shortly. Tia's next task was to check on some cleaning issues in the medical unit adjoining the one where Annette Richards had been killed. Reportedly, the grouting in one of the patient bathrooms was defective and as a result, there were deep stains around the base of the toilet and the edge of the sink. Tia had brought her own special cleaning supplies with her and her plan was to strip off the grouting herself and do the specialized cleaning and then call the maintenance man to replace it. Fortunately, the room was empty and would not be reoccupied for several days.

Tia entered the room and went straight to the bathroom. The situation was even worse than she had expected and she realized that some re-plastering would probably also be needed at the back of the sink. Also it was unclear if the deeply embedded stains at the base of the toilet could ever be removed without damaging the tile. However, she'd give it her best try. Sometimes 80% of a job well done was good enough in this environment where she'd gradually come to realize that perfection was often too much to ask! She called down to the maintenance man and explained what she was doing, saying that she would need him to come up at some point and consult with her on what would need to be done structurally to fix the situation. He agreed to come up presently and after hanging up, Tia opened her cleaning satchel and pulled out a scraper and some solvent, preparatory to removing the grouting. Then she heard a footfall and the sound of the bedroom door closing. She peeped out the bathroom door and saw Frankie Jessick standing there with a menacing look on his face. He reached into his pocket to pull something out and her heart dropped.

"It was you, wasn't it?" he demanded, taking several steps towards her and flashing a picture in her face. She only caught a quick glimpse but with a sinking heart she recognized Harrison's Cave and her own face looking out at her.

"I, uh, it's not what you think."

"You mean it's not like you're trying to pin Annette's murder on me? It's not that you're causing me to miss my plane and lose my ticket home? It's not like your actions are going to land me in jail for life?" He grabbed her shoulders and shoved her hard against the wall. Tia screamed involuntarily and just then the door opened.

"I had time now and ….Hey! What's going on?" the maintenance man demanded, lunging at Frankie.

"Nothing," Frankie sputtered. "We were just having a small disagreement."

"It didn't look small to me," Ed Carney said, wedging himself between Tia and Frank.

Tia was shaking. "He tried to kill me. He killed Annette! I'm calling the police and she reached for the phone in her purse."

"No!" Frank bellowed, and he snatched her purse out of her hands. But by this time people were gathering outside the door Ed had left open and somebody had called Security who in turn had called the police. Another orderly came in to assist Ed in subduing Frank who was violently struggling with him at this point. Within minutes, the police arrived and took him away.

"I didn't do it!" he screamed. "You're making a big mistake!"

The whole building was in an uproar at this point and Denise rushed in and took the trembling Tia in her arms. She helped her to the patient bed and sat down beside her on it with her arm behind Tia's back. Tia put her head between her knees and just tried to breathe. "It's over now," Denise said softly. "Just try to relax."

It took almost five minutes before Tia could stop shaking and begin to feel better. However, it wasn't to last for at that moment, Inspector McCoy came strutting in, having been notified on the police radio that there was an apparent breakthrough in one of his cases.

"Well," he said, unsympathetically, once he'd heard the story. "You see what happens when you try to take the law into your own hands!"

Tia said nothing.

"I think you've learned your lesson so I'll let you off with a warning this time but don't let it happen again," he snarled, and turned on his heel and walked out.

Denise had insisted on staying with Tia throughout the interrogation and now she just shook her head. "And I thought the police in Barbados were bad!" was all she could say.

Tia was coming back to herself. "I have to clean that bathroom," she said. "I need Ed to come back up here and figure out what repairs have to be done." He had left after Inspector McCoy had finished interviewing him and before he started in on Tia.

"Show me what you were planning to do and leave me the tools and I'll do it," Denise insisted. "You need to go home!"

"Okay," Tia said shakily, and led Denise into the bathroom. Use this to soften the grout and then this to scrape it off." Behind her, the current head of housekeeping had quietly entered and she said, "That's a maintenance job. You can't do that."

"But the new patient will be in here next week and we can't get the stains off properly until the grout is gone."

"I'll get Ed up here right now." Five minutes later, he was there and the three of them circled around Tia waiting for her sage advice on the onerous removal of these deep stains.

Tia looked at the three faces looking down at her as she crouched on the floor and tried a sample of one of her potions on the stain around the toilet. She felt a bit foolish and feared she'd end up looking like a fraud. But then she saw that the stain was lightening and she scrubbed at it vigorously with a Johnston's magic eraser. The stain came off in the small area she was working on and she breathed a sigh of relief. "Okay!" she said. "This is a three to one solution of potassium triphosphate, generally used in a more dilute form for cleaning walls before painting. Use rubber gloves and wear a mask for safety but it's not very toxic in small quantities. The stain is so bad here because mold has gotten into it. I suggest you just soak rags in the solution and drape them all around the base of the toilet. Then open the window and leave the bathroom, closing the door behind you. Half an hour later, go back and throw the towels in a pail full of water and with a cover to contain the smell. Then you should be able to rub the rest of the stain off with a magic eraser. When can you remove the grout, Ed?"

"I'll put the grout softener on now and come back later this afternoon to remove it. Same process as you suggest: open window and closed bathroom door because of the fumes. Denise, will you have time to do the cleaning tomorrow morning? If so, I can re-grout in the afternoon and it'll be all ready for the new occupant."

"Yes, I can do that," she said. Turning to Tia, she asked, "Now, will you go home?"

"Okay, I guess. But are you sure?"

Denise just snorted in response and the head housekeeper took Tia solicitously by her arm and asked if she could walk her to her car and if she felt strong enough to drive.

"That's not necessary, thanks," Tia said. "I'll be fine now—The threat is finally over."

Chapter 51—What Else Can Possibly Happen?

The outside air smelled crisp and clean and Tia filled her lungs with it as she walked slowly towards the parking lot. *What an adventure this was!* she thought, feeling vastly relieved that it was all over. But just then something zinged by her cheek, just touching it and tore into a tree beside her.

"Hey!" a man yelled, and he rushed towards her and slammed her into the ground. A second bullet whined over their heads and then they both heard footsteps thudding away. By the time they dared raise their heads to see, there was no one in evidence. The man flipped his phone out and with shaking fingers dialed 911. He reported their position and asked for help. Then he hung up and called hospital security. Even in her stunned state, Tia wondered at the order in which he'd done this. He looked at her quizzical face and said grimly, "We need to get to the bottom of this and it's beyond what the security guys can do. There's clearly a murderer loose at this institution!"

Tia was feeling woozy as the full impact of the situation hit her. *The murderer was still loose and Frank had been telling the truth!* she thought. *And now this person was after her!* At that point in her ruminations she just gave up and fainted.

When Tia came to, she found Denise standing over her with a grim face. "I called Jimmy and he's on his way," she said. "He's bringing somebody with him to drive your car back. I found his number in your purse," she added as an afterthought.

Tia just stared at her numbly and said nothing. Then she turned to the man who'd been her protector and thanked him. He introduced himself as Jake Urquhart, one of the visiting doctors who provided routine medical care for several of the Clive clients. Tia introduced herself and Denise in turn and smiled at him gratefully. But her smile faded when she saw Inspector McCoy once more stomping towards her. He was followed shortly after by a forensic team and they were all obliged to leave the area. They huddled in the Clive foyer which was just as well as Tia had begun once more to shake violently as the latest reaction set in. At that point, Jimmy and Claire came through the door. Jimmy put his arms around Tia and scowled at Inspector McCoy. Whether McCoy found this intimidating or whether he was finally able to muster up some sympathy for Tia since he really could not think of a way to blame her for this latest incident Tia did not know. But his questioning of her was surprisingly brief and gentle before he gave her permission to leave and turned his attention towards the doctor who'd pushed Tia down and a nurse who'd been walking by on the way to her car when she heard the shots. The nurse stated that she'd caught just a glimpse of a tall man racing away through the trees on the edge of the parking lot. McCoy did say to Tia before she left with Jimmy that he might need to talk to her further the next day. Tia said that she would be available since she had no intention of returning to the institution any time soon.

 Claire explained to Tia that Mario was already at her house and Dan was with him and would be taking him to school in the morning. She'd leave Tia's car at her house for the night and they could sort out the car delivery issue tomorrow. She left then and Jimmy settled Tia gently in the front seat of his car. She sat there numbly, still shaking a little, and he drove in silence. When he got to his home, Jimmy parked the car and opened the door for Tia.

"Aren't you going to take me home?"

"This is your home now," he responded tersely. "At least for tonight, you're not leaving my sight. He led her to his bedroom and handed her a clean, over-sized t-shirt and a new toothbrush. "Fortunately, I just changed the sheets a couple of days ago so they should be clean enough for you. Hurry up, because I'm coming in in five minutes." Fifteen minutes later, he was in bed with his arms tightly wrapped around her.

"Don't you want to hear what happened?"

"I know all I need to know. Some idiot is targeting you and you're not safe. Therefore, I'm not letting you out of my sight and Mario is going to stay with Claire and Dan until this is all over. The killer won't know to look for him there, just in case he's in danger, too!"

"Okay," Tia said, too exhausted to argue.

He clutched her more tightly and groaned. "You could have died tonight and we've never even known each other fully. No more. You're going to have to stop me now if you want to because I can't stop myself!" He kissed her then and ran his hands all over her body in almost a drunken frenzy. Tia did not stop him and some brief, intense moments of lovemaking followed—very brief and very intense. When it was over, he lay inertly with his head on her breast. "I'm sorry," he groaned. "It's been too long. I wanted our first time to be better than that."

"Don't be sorry," she said, stroking his hair gently. "I'm not. I needed that, too. Just to feel completely connected to you, to know that we belong to each other. But more than that I could not handle right now...I'm going to sleep," she added, groggily. Tia turned over and in seconds Jimmy heard her soft, even breathing.

Two minutes later he was also asleep, a slight smile playing on his face that had so often been surly in recent years.

Chapter 52——Starting All Over Again,

Claire was already sitting at the table with a cup of coffee and a bag of Tia's clothes when Tia shuffled into Jimmy's kitchen in her newly acquired t-shirt at nine the next morning. Claire grinned when she saw the t-shirt and the surprisingly peaceful look on Tia's face but only asked, "How are you this morning?"

"Much better," Tia responded.

"Jimmy had to go to work. I brought you some clothes".

"Thanks." Tia was rooting through Jimmy's cupboards looking for breakfast foods and commented, "I'm really hungry this morning for some reason." Claire did not respond but could not resist a faint smirk.

After they finished their coffee and Tia had eaten her toast and peanut butter, she started to review the previous day's events with Claire. By the time they finished talking and Tia had showered and dressed in her fresh clothes, it was eleven o'clock.

"Don't you need to get home?" Tia asked.

"No. Jessie's at school until 3:30 and I lost two new clients last week when I had to cancel for the second time because of Amy not coming at the last moment. Anyway, Jimmy made me promise to stay with you until he gets back. Dan is picking Mario up at school and they'll be back at home before Jessie arrives on the bus."

"Claire, if you're having a slow period right now, why don't you just take advantage of it to fire Amy?

You're never going to get anybody decent until you just bite the bullet and start from scratch!"

"You know what Dan says?" Claire mused.

"What?"

"He says I should just finish off with the couple of clients I have left and then stop for a while. He got that big contract he was after and that means he'll be out of town on frequent business trips and he says we don't need the money and my heart doesn't seem to be in it anyway or I'd have worked harder at solving the care issue. He thinks I should take a break and figure out what I really want to do. What do you think?"

Tia mulled through her thoughts before answering. A full minute passed before she responded and even then she spoke slowly as if still trying to work through what she wanted to say. "I think I know you pretty well at this point, Claire, and what I've observed is that you don't seem to be into this interior decorating business like you were—even a couple of years ago. Yeah, you still turn out beautiful designs but I don't see you putting in that zest and creative energy you used to have. And," Tia added, "I've often wondered why you even became an interior decorator in the first place since you aren't exactly that obsessed with cleaning and organizing!"

"Yeah, you are right," Claire sighed. "I've found it way more exciting to organize the home for Jimmy and Mavis and Roscoe than any decorating project I've ever done. It just seems more meaningful somehow."

"Then why did you ever go in for a decorating career in the first place?"

"Well," Claire said, defensively, "I *am* artistically inclined—and I wasn't exactly encouraged or supported to get more than a basic B.A. at university!" She thought for a moment and then added, "That's not all, I suppose. I think I was always trying to get back the home I had before my mother died. It was so beautiful before and after, when that woman came, my stepmother, it was always messy and dusty and ugly, somehow. Just like our life then. And every time I create a beautiful room and admire it after I finish it, it seems to me like for a little while I have undone that ugliness. Then I walk away and I keep that picture in my mind, the way it was when I left each home for the last time after my work was completed, and I guess I feel kind of powerful and right and even like I made the world a little better by creating some beauty and order in a little corner of it. And I suppose after I'm gone it gradually gets a little messy and taken for granted and kind of lived in. But I hope it never gets like my mother's house got."

Tia sat quietly, listening to her friend, and she observed a small tear slipping out of the corner of Claire's eye. Claire went on speaking, "And then there's Jessie. There are things to do for her all the time quite apart from her daily care. There are meetings with the school personnel and therapists and with her social worker to monitor what's happening at home. There are all her special meals to make and specialist visits and equipment changes and hiring staff. And then I look around my house and some days I feel like I have just fallen back into the same nightmare I had growing up. Jessie's stuff all over the place, dust, disorder, never having everything done, always depending on some teenage girl to show up when she says she will. Amy is not the only one who's ever let me down, you know." Claire stopped speaking for a minute and then she added in a quieter voice, "Some days I just feel useless and kind of hopeless."

Tia looked at her friend whom she admired so much and just shook her head sorrowfully. "That's not right. Something has to be done!" Tia was quiet for a moment and then proceeded very slowly and carefully. "You know what I think? I think Dan is right. You should stop the decorating right now, but I don't think you should do nothing. I've been talking to Denise and she really does not want the team leader job. She does not want to give up the benefits she gets at the hospital and I'm not sure I want to give up the hospital work entirely either. Denise says she would really like to do a couple of shifts a week at the home just as something extra but she'd like to continue to work maybe four days a week at the hospital. You've already done so much for Bill and for all of us. We never would have got that house or have been able to get this far this fast with PDD without you. I think *you* should be the team leader! *And,"* Tia added enticingly, "You can use the house staff as a relief pool when Jessie's aid is not available! I bet some of them would like the chance to work in a different setting and with a younger person occasionally, when they are not working in the home. I know Denise would like that chance!"

Claire looked at Tia stunned. "Do you really think so?" she asked. "I know how I've been feeling inside. I haven't felt so alive and powerful in a long time and I have loved every single step of it, even though it's been tense and scary at times. I guess when I stop to think about it, what I really have loved is the chance to try to make their lives right. Maybe I wish somebody would have tried harder to make my life right."

Tia moved over to sit beside her friend and put her arms around her. "Just think about it," she said softly. "I don't want to bulldoze you but it seems right to me."

"I will," Claire said, "and I'll talk to Dan tonight. And Jessie, too!" she added. "Sometimes when I'm really confused about something, I just hold her on my lap and talk to her and rock her back and forth and stroke her hand and it seems like she understands. And

I always feel calmer then and the answers start to come!"

They sat calmly then for a few minutes until Tia started and asked, "Is today Thursday?"

"Yes," Claire nodded.

"Oh," Tia exclaimed, "With everything that's been happening, I almost forgot. Mario has a Scout meeting tonight and I need to get his uniform from the house!"

"Mario is going to Scouts? It doesn't seem like his kind of thing!"

"He doesn't want to go. He says he wants to avoid 'group think'—and my parents are supporting him on that. They told him all about the fascist youth groups during the war in Italy and how they were just a forum for brainwashing young people. They believe Scouts is just like that!"

"Well, why are you making him go then?"

"Because he needs to learn how to get along with others and work as part of a team and he has to broaden his interests and become well-rounded. It doesn't really matter how smart you are. If you can't work as part of a team you aren't going to get very far in this world!"

Claire just shook her head, and remembering how Mario was, she could not keep a faint smile from her lips. She was pretty sure he'd work this dilemma out to his satisfaction and it was not her place to interfere so she just said cheerfully, "Okay, I'll drive you over there whenever you're ready."

"I can go myself," Tia said, faintly irritated.

"No, I promised Jimmy not to leave you alone."

Chapter 53—Where There Is Smoke...

As Claire pulled up in front of Tia's house, her cell phone rang. She glanced at the caller id and saw that it was from Jessie's school. "I need to take this," she said with a worried frown.

"Okay. I'm just going to run in and grab Mario's outfit fast in case you need to leave right away. I'm also going to do a quick check on the back gate. The latch is loose and sometimes the gate swings open." Tia opened the door and walked quickly around the house. She was relieved to see that the back gate was still firmly shut but when she turned and approached the back door her worries returned. It was slightly ajar and she heard a scuffing sound inside. *Had an animal got in?* she wondered. Tia opened the door slowly and peeked inside. Then she gasped in horror! A woman was methodically sprinkling gas from a red gas can all over the kitchen floor. When the woman saw Tia, she rushed at her and grabbed her firmly, dragging her inside.

"Great timing!" she grated out, glaring at Tia with crazed eyes. "It'll be much more satisfying to burn you and your house together instead of your house alone!" She threw Tia to the floor, holding her down by stepping firmly on her back and grabbed a big knife from the nearby kitchen knife block. Tia looked at her fearfully. "Oh, don't worry, I'm not going to stab you with this," she said. "It'll be much more fun to think of you burning alive. I always liked that Joan of Arc story!"

"What did I ever do to you?" Tia gasped—and then she finally recognized her. It was Jennie, the LPN from Bill's unit at the Clive Centre where Annette Richards had been killed!

"You know what you did!" Jennie snarled. "Coming to Clive and pretending to be a housekeeper just so you could snoop around. And then getting poor Frank arrested. Annette *deserved* what she got—and it was none of your business, anyway!" As she said this, Jennie was slicing the long cords from Tia's coffee pot and toaster. Like all the other appliances in the small kitchen they were older models, crafted before long cords had been perceived as a safety threat and before they were encased in a plastic cover. Although Tia squirmed mightily as Jennie was doing this, she could not extricate herself. Jennie did not have to reach very far in Tia's small kitchen to do these tasks. She then knelt on Tia with her full weight, one knee on her neck and the other on her thighs and wrapped the first cord tightly around Tia's hands before repeating the process on her feet with the second cord.

"Help!" Tia yelled loudly.

As she said this, Jennie was pouring gasoline on the dish cloth and swabbing it around Tia's face and neck. "Shut up, if you don't want this cloth stuffed in your mouth. That could give a whole new meaning to 'burning your tongue'!" As she said this, she cackled loudly and almost demonically. Tia wondered briefly about Jennie's mental health but then refocused on her own dire situation. Jennie sloshed the rest of the gas in the can over Tia's body and then up and down the walls. She threw the can down, backed towards the door and pulled out a package of matches.

"No-o-o!" Tina screamed, wondering frantically where Claire was. At that moment, the door burst open violently, knocking Jennie back against the wall and causing her to drop the matches. Claire quickly sized up the situation, grabbed Tia by the feet and hauled her out through the open door, bumping her down the back steps. They heard a mighty scream from inside and then the kitchen burst into flames and Jennie ran out the door, passed them and ran out the back gate. Only then did Claire notice the small car parked in the back alley behind Tia's neighbor's house. Claire frantically pulled Tia further back into the dirt of the back garden, reasoning that if Tia should catch fire from a random spark Claire could roll her in the dirt to put it out. She was trying to get the knots in the cords binding Tia undone but not succeeding very well. They were the old fashioned kind covered with cloth rather than rubber so the knots did not slip and Jennie had tied them very tightly. Just as they heard the whine of the fire siren, a spark lit up Tia's back. Claire frantically clawed at the partially frozen dirt, tossing it ineffectually on Tia to douse the growing flames and then in desperation, beating at them with her hands. There was a great whooshing sound and the sound of breaking windows and, more faintly, the sound of another siren in the background. Claire felt suddenly wet and turned to see a fireman playing a powerful stream of water up and down Tia's inert form. The entire scene was surreal and Claire was no longer sure of what she was seeing. 'Were two policemen coming through the back gate with Jennie? What were those big white bubbles on her hands? Was that another siren?' Suddenly, two paramedics were there, checking Tia's pulse and then lifting her gently onto a stretcher before hurrying away with her. In a couple of minutes, one was back and took Claire by the elbow, helping her to her feet and guiding her gently towards the ambulance.

"No, I need to go to my daughter's school. The occupational therapist is there and wants to talk to me about her feeding program!"

"Give me the number and I'll call your school but you're coming with us," he said.

Claire handed him her phone numbly, saying, "It's the last call on there. You can just redial." Then she fainted.

"I need help here!" the EMT (Emergency Medical Technician) bellowed. A fireman came to his assistance and between them, they got Claire into the front seat of the ambulance. The EMT hopped in the back with Tia and the ambulance took off, siren screaming.

Chapter 54—the End of the Road

Claire awoke on the way to the hospital and asked immediately about Tia.

"Your friend should be alright. Her vital signs are good."

"And her burns?"

"Don't know. We're not allowed to touch them or remove her clothing to check. But we do know that she had on a cotton shirt and sweater so that's a good thing."

"Because?"

"Because synthetics melt," he replied grimly.

Claire stared at him in horror. "Is she awake?"

"We've given her a strong sedative. It's best not to try to talk to her right now."

When they got to the Emergency Unit at the hospital, Tia was whisked away immediately for emergency treatment and Claire was taken to one of the curtained-off little rooms and examined by a nurse. Both the palms and the backs of her hands had second and third degree burns from her frantic efforts to beat out the flames on Tia's back and she was coughing badly from smoke inhalation. Her hands were treated with a sterilizing silver and mercury solution to protect against infection and promote healing and then bandaged with special, non-adhering pads and covered with gauze. She was given a strong pain killer and a shot of anti-biotic and left to sleep and rest as best she could in the little cubicle. When she awoke it was to find Dan, Jessie and Aunt Gus all staring down at her.

Dan's face was a battleground of conflicting emotions. Claire saw love, concern and anger there—all at war with each other. "I'm innocent!" she blurted. "All we were trying to do was to pick up Mario's Scout uniform."

"But there was a reason Tia was not staying at the house in the first place, if you recall," Dan pointed out.

"It was still daylight and it was just supposed to be for a minute. I stayed in the car because the school called. I only went to check when Tia did not come back." Claire reached out to stroke Jessie's hand and winced in pain. Jessie felt the touch of the gauze and started to fuss, realizing something was wrong.

Aunt Gus weighed in at this point, rocking Jessie's chair gently as she had seen Claire do many times. "I'm moving in until you can manage on your own—to look after you and help look after Jessie. You can tell me what to do and I'll be your hands." Gus had carefully avoided looking at Dan when she spoke but her voice was firm and held genuine care and concern. Of course, at the back of her mind, she could not help thinking that this would be an opportunity to score some much needed Brownie points with Dan and to reassure Claire that she could be trusted to care for Jessie.

Claire sneaked a peek at Dan's face and saw the conflict there. She knew that Aunt Gus irritated him and that he was still upset about the two times she'd inadvertently placed Jessie's life at risk. However, she also knew that he was in the midst of a big project with deadlines looming. He must realize that her temporarily useless hands left them with a huge dilemma, given the amount of intensive, hands-on care that Jessie required.

An awkward moment of silence followed before Dan finally spoke. "That would be very helpful, Gus," he said gruffly. "Thank you."

Claire glanced at Aunt Gus just in time to see her shoulders drop. *She must have been feeling very tense and uncertain when she made that offer*, Claire thought, not knowing how it would be received. "Thank you, Aunt Gus. We could really use your help right now, particularly with feeding Jessie and dressing her. The doctor said I have to be very careful not to stretch the skin on the back of my hands until it heals."

"I can help with toileting, too, you know. I'm no prude. I'll learn how to use that ceiling lift of yours—safely," she added, looking at Dan for emphasis. Jessie began to fuss at this point, causing Gus to wince. Beneath her apparent shallowness and self-centeredness lurked a great fear of rejection.

"The doctor said you need to stay here overnight so she can be sure there's no infection setting into your hands but I'll be back about eleven tomorrow morning," Dan interjected. "After she sees you, if everything is okay, I can take you home. I'll bring you fresh clothes and take the ones you were wearing today home to wash. They must reek of smoke!" Dan kissed Claire gently on the forehead and they left.

Meanwhile, down the hall, a different scene was unfolding. Mario and Jimmy sat quietly beside Tia's bed waiting for her to awaken from the anesthetic. The burn on her back had been sufficiently severe that the dead skin had to be scraped away, a very painful procedure. As Tia started to awaken, a nurse arrived to give her a shot of strong painkiller. Lana, as the name on her id card stated, addressed them then. "Your wife is going to be in a lot of pain for the next 48 hours at least. It will be best if we keep her heavily sedated but you can talk to her for a few minutes now. Then you will need to leave her alone to rest."

Tia opened her eyes then and looked groggily at them but the nurse was still fussing around, asking her how she was feeling and taking her blood pressure and temperature. Finally, it looked like she was leaving. "Do the 'few minutes' start now?" Jimmy asked with the old surly note back in his voice.

"You can have 15 minutes," she said, and left.

"Why?" Jimmy asked, with a combination of sorrow, fear and anger on his face, eyes glistening with unshed tears. "Why did you go there?"

"Mario's uniform," Tia croaked. "Scout meeting." She noticed Mario, for the first time, sitting back from the bed and swathed in a white coat and mask like the ones Jimmy was wearing. He looked very young and vulnerable and frightened and was uncharacteristically silent. "Mario, don't worry. I'll be alright. Aunty Claire put the fire out right away. I could feel her beating on my back with her bare hands." Silent tears slipped down Tia's cheeks when she said this.

Jimmy slipped his arm around Mario's thin shoulders and squeezed him hard. "We can't even give you a hug," he groaned. "The doctor said a strict protocol must be maintained because of the high danger of infection."

Tia's eyes were heavy and it was obvious she was fighting to keep awake. "The house!" she moaned. "What about the house?"

"The kitchen is toast, the living room is a mess but the bedrooms are intact. Your office is in the basement as I recall so it should be okay. There's a lot of smoke and water damage everywhere, of course," Jimmy replied.

"How long until they can fix it?" she cried.

"It doesn't matter," Jimmy said angrily, "because you're never going to live there again. I'm going down to city hall to apply for a marriage license and as soon as you're out of here you're coming to live with me. Mario is moving in tonight and we're going to start planning how to fix up his bedroom." Jimmy gave Mario another squeeze at this point and then he added, "And I don't give a damn about the church. We can sort the annulment thing out later and if that doesn't work, we can just become Protestants. To Hell with them all, anyway!" he finished angrily.

Tia gave a faint smile. "Okay," she said meekly, and she saw a glimmer of a smile on Mario's face for the first time. The nurse came in then and ushered them out.

Chapter 55—Life Moves On

It was two weeks later and Tia had only been home, at Jimmy's house, for a couple of days. She moved stiffly in bed, adjusting the pillows that were propped under her to keep her in a reasonably comfortable position, half on her side and half on her stomach. This was the position that put the least pressure on her back. It was still early and Jimmy had not yet brought the sheets and blankets in from the sofa where he was spending his nights now that she was back. This was not out of any sense of propriety but rather out of concern that if they shared the same bed he might accidentally touch her back and hurt it, or worse still infect it.

The doorbell rang and Claire arrived. Her left hand was free now with only a three-inch by two-inch gauze bandage loosely applied to the back of it. She went into the bedroom to talk to Tia but did not touch her. They were still maintaining a strict protocol and Claire was now driving Tia back and forth to the hospital every day to get the bandages changed as Jimmy was back at work. "Hi, Claire," Tia said. "I'll be ready to go in a few minutes."

"You better eat something first," Claire responded, looking at her friend with concern. Tia had lost 15 pounds during her hospital stay and was looking very thin and frail. "We have time," Claire continued, "I came early."

"Why's that?" Tia asked, gingerly pulling some loose sweat pants up to her waist and buttoning a baggy cardigan over her upper body.

Sergeant Crombie phoned last night. He wants to come over tonight and tell us what Jennie told them about why she did what she did.

"I really need to know," Tia groaned, "but the house is a mess. There's dust everywhere and the kitchen floor has not been washed in almost three weeks."

"Don't worry," Claire said smugly. "It's all being taken care of."

"Don't tell me *you're* going to clean it!" Tia said, disbelievingly.

"Oh no, I know you'd never be satisfied. I'm bringing in some experts, trained by the best!" Tia raised her eyebrows, one part of her that did not hurt. Claire continued, "Jimmy asked me to collect all your business papers and anything else of value from your house just in case there was a break-in. I found your client list and called a few of the old timers you've worked with for a long time. I told them what had happened and how laid up you were and that the house really needed attention. Janice organized a cleaning bee with three of your other clients and they're all coming today at eleven to do up the house. And don't worry. They're bringing their own equipment, the good stuff you urged them to get, so you don't need to be here to tell them where anything is. I promised that we'd be out of here well before eleven since that's the time of your dressing change and they figure they'll be done by one with the four of them working together. Janice assured me they'll know exactly what to do, having watched you in action for so long so don't worry about it."

Tia sat down gingerly in a chair but she really did not know what to say. She was more used to giving than receiving. Her clients knew this, of course. That's why they did not want to hang around waiting to be thanked and Janice had made Claire promise to keep Tia out of the house while they were there. "What about my own cleaning supplies, and my cleaning satchel? Are they okay?" was all Tia said.

"Yes, I rescued them, too, as well as your vacuum cleaner—*and* your favorite mop. I knew you would not want to lose that!" Tia smiled at this and Claire, taking that as a yes, called up Sergeant Crombie and arranged for him to arrive at 7:30 that evening. "He assured me several times over that he did not want to come for dinner and *we're* bringing dessert so don't even think about that!" Claire said.

"Who are *we*? Is Gus coming with you?"

"No. Dan is!" Claire said happily.

"You're going to leave Jessie alone with *Gus?*"

"Jessie's assistant will be there until nine and she will put Jessie to bed before she leaves. All Aunt Gus will have to do is stay nearby to make sure Jessie is okay. She knows what to do if Jessie has a seizure or throws up or aspirates on her saliva and it turns out that she is surprisingly strong and wiry. According to her, she's been doing Pilates and weight lifting for years!"

"I'm surprised she was willing to pass up a chance to get the scoop directly from Sergeant Crombie. I remember how eager she was last time!" Tia commented.

"She has really changed, you know," Claire said. She talked to me yesterday when Dan wasn't around. She said I should take him along because maybe he would be a little more sympathetic to our adventures if he could hear directly from Sergeant Crombie how much good we were doing."

"But we didn't do anything *this* time. Our trip to Barbados was just a red herring and revealing Jennie as the killer was just a fluke—me being in the wrong place at the wrong time and you, by sheer accident, having to remain in the car and make that phone call so later you were free to call the police before she saw you, once you figured out what was happening." Tia paused for a moment and then went on. "Wait a minute! How *did* you know what was happening before you came in there?"

"I smelled the gas first. Then I got this funny feeling. I'd been about to call out, but instead I peeked through the door and I saw you on the floor and Jennie pouring gas on you. I just stepped back and called 911 and asked for police and fire assistance. Fortunately, I knew your address by heart and I told them quickly what was happening and then hung up. I crept back to the door, calculated where she was and slammed the door against her when she was in the right position so I'd have a moment to haul you out."

"Not your usual impulsive style, all that thinking ahead," Tia commented.

"I know. I guess all Dan's haranguing through the years paid off. As bad as the situation was, I knew I had to take that moment to think it through and call for help and not try to play the hero single handed."

"Well, you were pretty heroic just the same!" Tia said softly, and she picked up Claire's bandaged hand and kissed it.

Claire smiled affectionately at her friend and said "Jennie would have gotten completely away with killing Annette if we had not drawn her out through our investigative efforts, particularly yours. And Bill would have had the suspicion of being a murderer hanging over him for the rest of his life!"

"Okay, fine. Maybe it will be a good thing having Dan there. But I still don't see why Gus suggested it. She's not known for her empathy!"

"Like I said, she is *really* changing, Tia. In fact, I don't know how I'd have managed without her these past two weeks. You can't do much when you can't use your hands and even when I put on rubber gloves over the bandages I still can't manage much beyond swilling out a couple of tea cups. There's too much danger of the scabs breaking open if I put pressure on my hands. Once the skin heals over enough so there's no more danger of infection and the bandages can come off, I'll start putting Biotin and Tea Oil on them to help keep the new skin flexible and elastic—and we'll do the same to your back. That's also supposed to reduce the scarring."

"I'm so sorry about your hands," Tia said softly. "If I hadn't been so obsessed about Mario not missing Scouts, none of this would have happened."

"And then maybe we never would have caught the killer."

"Well, anyway, I didn't mean to change the subject. I want to know more about how Gus has changed."

"She's virtually taken over feeding Jessie—and she is actually pretty good at it, seems to have a knack. Of course, now I have to put up with her talking to me in patronizing tones about how it should be done, how you have to hold Jessie's head at just the right angle and wait until she's ready to put the spoon in her mouth so she won't choke. As if I did not *know* that! Oh, and she quickly learned how to use the lift and the lifting sling correctly and she even positions Jessie properly in her wheelchair and on the commode so she's not sitting on the base of her spine or slumped over to one side because of her scoliosis. A lot of the assistants I've had have never figured that out completely, not even after they've been with Jessie for months!"

"Wow! That's impressive! But why do you think she's changed? She's always seemed so self-centered and uninterested in other people."

"I don't think she really has changed. What I think is she's never really found herself, never managed to fit herself in somewhere where she felt she had a significant role to play. That seems to happen to some people—and then they develop defenses to protect their self-esteem. I think that's why she's so into fitness and controlling her weight and dressing so smartly. She wants to look younger and fitter and more elegant and attractive than her contemporaries. That allows her to feel like she wins and is significant in some ways at least."

"But she isn't very attractive and I've heard Dan say that as well. She has a narrow face and her eyes are kind of small and her skin is sallow and she has plenty of wrinkles. How can she even delude herself like that?"

"I know, and you forgot to even mention her hair—the family curse!" Claire said, patting her own limp, flat mop. But she can look quite attractive when she wants to, between her hair pieces and her false eyelashes and make-up and she really does have some striking and tasteful clothing items and accessories. Anyway, I would never say those things you just said to her. Even Dan has never been so angry or so cruel as to point those things out. I think we both realize that she's very fragile underneath her layers of illusion and it would be destructive to try to tear her vanity away from her."

"Wow. You're sounding more like a psychologist than an interior designer!"

"I don't know about that—but I do seem to be more interested in people than in furniture these days."

"Does that mean you would be willing to take on the team leader position? Remember, we were discussing it before the fire?" Tia held her breath.

"Yes, to start with at least. We will see what happens. Actually, doing the interior design for a home for three people with such different disabilities presents a very interesting challenge in itself—and I intend to be in charge of that!" Claire ended, warningly.

"But we have already done most of the renovations."

"I mean furniture choice and arrangement, free flowing to allow ample wheelchair access for Mavis and furniture pieces safe for Roscoe who has an unstable gait due to his low muscle tone, characteristic of Down Syndrome. I also want to create a harmonious order and simplicity in the furniture arrangement so we won't be tempted to move things around and upset Bill who, as you know, finds any change very upsetting. Home design for persons with disabilities is a whole area of interior design that has yet to be explored. If we want to include these people in the mainstream then we better make the mainstream accessible psychologically as well as physically!"

Tia smiled happily at the enthusiasm evident in Claire's voice, but had to ask, "What about their other needs, a daily activity program, for example?"

"Don't worry. I've been thinking a lot about that as well. My first task will be to find a suitable work placement for Roscoe. I think he needs something like that and is smart enough to handle it. And I have some ideas about how to improve Bill's and Mavis' life as well—but I'll tell you about them another day!"

Epilogue

Sergeant Crombie arrived promptly at 7:30 that evening and once he had greeted everyone and was comfortably settled with some coffee and cake, he began talking. "From her medical and school records we know that Jennie Marlowe had some learning difficulties at school and it took her a long time to get through her LPN program. She also has some emotional problems. As a teenager she was hospitalized twice and placed on suicide watch because of severe depression and in recent years she has also had some bouts of hypomania. She's supposed to be on medication but does not always take it. Her job at the Clive Centre is the longest bout of employment she's had and of course they did not know about her emotional problems when they hired her.

According to what Jennie told us, when Frankie Jessick first arrived at Clive he was interested in her and they dated a couple of times. But then he started spending more time with Annette and seemed to lose interest in Jennie. She believed Annette had deliberately stolen him away from her and that if she got rid of Annette she could get Frankie back. That's why she killed her and tried to frame Bill. What Frankie told us was that he was never really interested in Jennie and did not particularly like her once he got to know her better. He just spent some time with her at the beginning because he was lonely. When he realized that Annette was working at the hospital, he focused on her, first so he could find out where she lived so that he could kill her when she was away from the hospital and be less likely to become a suspect. But as he got to know her better he changed his mind. He realized that she was being appropriately punished for her sins, trapped in an unhappy marriage. What he did want from her, though, was to find out all he could about what his brother had been thinking and feeling during the time that Marvin and Annette were so close. Annette did finally admit to him that she felt guilty over his brother's death and realized that she had made a mistake in leaving him. Frankie felt like this gave him back his brother a little and helped him to move on from his grief."

"But why did he attack Tia, then?" Jimmy asked.

"He told us he really just wanted to talk to her, to tell her his story and to let her know that she was creating more grief for him just when he was starting to heal and how unfair he thought that was."

"Well, he was the obvious suspect," Claire said. "I guess we fell into Inspector McCoy's trap, ourselves, of jumping to conclusions."

"But why did Jennie try to kill me—and in such a diabolical way?" Tia asked. She was ensconced in a large armchair with pillows placed strategically around her and still moving very slowly and gingerly.

Sergeant Crombie looked at her sorrowfully. "It never should have happened," he said. "If we'd done thorough background checks we would have found out about her mental illness and probably about her attraction to Frankie early on. And, of course, we would have found out about Frankie's brother. You would not have needed to go to Barbados to find a lead and none of this would have happened to you. Have you thought about registering a complaint against how this case was handled? I know Inspector McCoy can say that you should not have been interfering and were specifically warned not to do that. However, what happened to Bill as a result was not something you could have any control over and you could complain on his behalf."

Claire and Tia were surprised. They'd never heard the ever-patient Sergeant Crombie speak so directly against McCoy before. They could see he was very upset by the damage that had been done to both of them by the fire and particularly to Tia. Tia said softly, "I'm not interested in vengeance. And it's not as if Inspector McCoy is educable. If we end up on opposite sides again he'll still be clinging to his prejudices and narrow mindedness. And *he is* vengeful. I don't want to cross him. I basically don't want anything more to do with him if I can possibly avoid it."

Claire spoke then. "You know, for all the grief he has caused us, some good *did* come out of it. We would not have had to buy the house and set up our own system for Mavis and Bill and Roscoe otherwise, and I think their lives and ours will ultimately be better because we were forced into that action plan. So as far as I'm concerned, I say let sleeping dogs lie. He's the one who has to deal with his conscience, assuming he has one. Oh, and don't go telling him he did us any favors, Sergeant Crombie. Let him bear the full weight of his actions. That is *my* revenge!"

THE END

About the Author

In her private life, Emma and her husband, Joe Pivato, have raised three children, the youngest, Alexis, having multiple challenges. Their efforts to organize the best possible life for her have provided some of the background context for this book. The society they formed to support Alexis in her adult years is described at http://www.homewithinahome.com/Main.html.

Emma's first cozy mystery and first in her Claire Burke series is entitled *Blind Sight Solution*.

List of Acronyms

CARP—Canadian Association of Retired Persons—"CARP is a national, non-partisan, non-profit organization committed to a 'New Vision of Aging for Canada' promoting social change that will bring financial security, equitable access to health care and freedom from discrimination." http://www.carp.ca/about-carp/ (Retrieved January 14, 2014)

AACL—Alberta Association of Community Living—"Alberta Association for Community Living (AACL) is a family based, non-profit federation that advocates on behalf of children and adults with developmental disabilities and their families". http://www.aacl.org/ (retrieved January 14, 2014)

PDD—Persons with Developmental Disabilities— "PDD funds programs and services to help adult Albertans with developmental disabilities to be a part of their communities and live as independently as they can" http://humanservices.alberta.ca/disability-services/pdd.html (retrieved January 14th, 2014)

AADL—Alberta Aids to Daily Living—"The Alberta Aids to Daily Living (AADL) program helps Albertans with a long-term disability, chronic illness or terminal illness to maintain their independence at home, in lodges or group homes by providing financial assistance to buy medical equipment and supplies." http://www.health.alberta.ca/services/aids-to-daily-living.html (retrieved January 14, 2014)

Endnotes

[i] Bruce Uditsky has been Chief Executive Officer of Albert Association for Community Living for more than two decades. During his tenure AACL has become a powerful advocacy organization, supporting people with developmental disabilities throughout Alberta.

[ii] http://www.alexisenterprisesltd.com/HOME.html Please see this website for further information on the wheelchair with a built-in lift and built-in commode unit.

[iii] Jean Paré, a caterer from Vermilion, Alberta, has created more than twenty different cookbooks in her "*Company's Coming*" series. These are now sold around the world and her culinary enterprise has become a big business involving many of her family members. She tests every recipe on her family before including them in her books. The cakes mentioned here are taken from her cake cookbook.

Made in the USA
Monee, IL
08 June 2021